D1143112

As they danced, Liv could almost feel the tension draining out of him, replaced by something else—something more vibrant and compelling.

She moved her hands from where they were linked around his neck, placing them on his chest, startled to feel the unsteady thud of his heart beneath her palms. A gravelly fractured sigh escaped him.

'This feels so good, doesn't it, Livvy?'

She tipped her head back, meeting the dark caress of his eyes. All at once she felt the slow heat between their bodies flaring, engulfing her. And time shot backwards so that it seemed only yesterday when they had been so young, so in love.

Husband and wife…

Leah Martyn loves to create warm, believable characters for the medical series. She is grounded firmly in rural Australia, and the special qualities of the bush are reflected in her stories. For plots and possibilities she bounces ideas off her husband on their early-morning walks. Browsing in bookshops and buying an armful of new releases is high on her list of enjoyable things to do.

Recent titles by the same author:

THE BUSH DOCTOR'S RESCUE
DR CHRISTIE'S BRIDE

THE SURGEON'S MARRIAGE RESCUE

BY
LEAH MARTYN

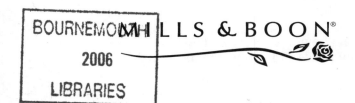

MILLS & BOON®

First published in Great Britain 2006
Large Print edition 2006
Harlequin Mills & Boon Limited,
Eton House, 18-24 Paradise Road,
Richmond, Surrey TW9 1SR

© Leah Martyn 2006

ISBN-13: 978 0 263 19526 2
ISBN-10:   0 263 19526 0

Set in Times Roman 16¾ on 20 pt.
17-1006-50078

Printed and bound in Great Britain
by Antony Rowe Ltd, Chippenham, Wiltshire

CHAPTER ONE

'How are things, kiddo?' Adam Westerman strolled out onto the sunlit verandah and addressed his young patient. Cancer survivor Jade McKinney had recently had her left leg amputated above the knee. But she was all high spirits and sparkling eyes as she turned from where she'd been looking out through the windows at the Sydney city skyline.

'Things are good, Dr Adam.' The youngster scooted towards him on her crutches. 'I'm going home.'

Adam raised a dark brow. Well, that piece of information had certainly got out fast. The decision to discharge Jade had been made barely thirty minutes earlier.

'Dr Sally told me.'

Adam stifled a wry laugh. Sally Ryder was

the third member of their surgical team at St Christopher's and had bonded closely with Jade during her weeks of hospitalisation.

And even though he was the senior doctor, Adam certainly wasn't going to hold it against Sally that she'd taken it on herself to give their young patient the news she'd been so longing to hear.

'I've just spoken to your mum,' Adam told Jade. 'She's off down to the travel agent to arrange your flight home.'

'Uh-huh.' Jade wrinkled her small freckled nose thoughtfully. 'But I think we might have to wait a couple of days to catch a flight to Bellreagh.'

'Is that where you're from?' Adam felt a moment of pure heart-pumping astonishment. He'd known Jade was a country kid: a large percentage of their juvenile patients needing specialised surgery were.

But Bellreagh…?

Suddenly, memories of his home town were intruding, buzzing around his head like bees disturbed from their hive.

'We're having our hundred-year celebrations in

a few weeks' time.' Jade wheeled expertly on her crutches and plonked herself down on the padded arm of one of the colourful sofas that dotted the enclosed verandah. 'That should be really cool.'

'I'm sure it will,' Adam said softly, and wondered why Josh hadn't told him anything about the upcoming events. But, then, lately his son hadn't seemed to have time to tell him much about anything.

Sadness darkened Adam's eyes for a second. Being divorced and an absentee father were the pits. He would really have to talk to Liv about having access to their son much more frequently…

'Why don't you come?'

'Sorry?' Adam looked startled.

Jade sent him an old-fashioned look. 'You were daydreaming.'

'I suppose I was.' Adam's laugh was rough, and forced. 'What was the question again?'

'I asked you to come to Bellreagh's centenary celebrations. You could, couldn't you?'

Adam scraped a hand across his cheekbones. Hell, what an idea! He could take time off—the hospital certainly owed him plenty, and it would be quality time he could spend with his son.

'If you came, I could see you at the hospital to have my check-up instead of having to come back to Sydney.'

'You could at that.' Adam's look was wry. He was being outgunned by this feisty little thirteen-year-old. But the fact remained. He *could* co-ordinate Jade's check-up with a visit to Bellreagh. Suddenly, the whole idea began to take shape.

His interest now well and truly ignited, Adam asked, 'So, when exactly is all this happening, young Jade? Do you have the dates?'

As if she sensed a victory, Jade hopped to her feet. 'The kids from school sent me a couple of flyers about the celebrations and stuff. I'll just get one from my locker.' She was back in a flash, the bright yellow flyer tucked safely under her arm. 'The yellow is supposed to rep-resent the wattles, I think.' She propped herself on her crutches and handed Adam the leaflet. 'They'll be out in bloom for the festival.'

Memories as sharp as glass hit Adam. Just as

quickly he shrugged them away, skimming over the list of simple country pleasures that were being offered to celebrate the town's centenary.

There was to be a dinner-dance on the Friday evening, a sports day on the Saturday, featuring a tug-of-war contest between two teams made up from staff at the hospital. Adam smiled faintly. *That* should be interesting—or hilarious, depending on your point of view. A combined church service and craft market, in that order, were listed for the Sunday, the final day of the celebrations.

'It should be fun,' Jade reinforced, her fair head tilted at a pert little angle. 'I'll be getting used to my new leg by then, too, so I won't have to miss out on anything.' A wry smile tickled the side of her mouth. 'Except I might be a bit slow in the three-legged race.'

Adam's huff of laughter was spontaneous. He wanted to hug this gutsy kid for rising so gallantly above the rotten deal she'd been handed, when she could so easily have drowned under its weight.

Suddenly, his own dissatisfaction with his personal life appeared pathetic and shallow. He needed to stop wallowing in self-pity and do something to change things, meet life's shortcomings full on, the way Jade had done. Hell, she set an example he could only aspire to.

'OK, you've talked me into it, clever clogs. If I can arrange the time off, I'll be there.'

'Excellent!' Palm up, Jade offered a high-five salute to seal their deal.

'I'll be in contact with your mum about arranging a time for your check-up while I'm in Bellreagh.' Adam laid a reassuring hand on his young patient's shoulder. 'Now, anything you want to ask me before you go home?'

'Don't think so.' Jade chewed on her lip for a second and then said slowly, 'Sometimes…it feels like my leg is still there.'

Adam nodded. 'That's pretty normal. Is it bothering you a lot?'

'Not really. Last night it felt as though my missing foot was itchy so I just scratched the other one and it was fine.'

'Good girl.' Adam's look was soft. Lord, the child was an inspiration. 'I'll see you in a few weeks' time, then.' He moved his hand, letting it rest briefly on the back of Jade's fine silky head. 'Take care, sweetheart.'

'Hey, guys, I hear both the pubs and the motels are fully booked for the centenary celebrations.' Charge nurse Mike Townsend addressed the company who had arrived for the late shift at Bellreagh district hospital.

'And apparently the caravan park is at bursting point as well,' Suzy Barker chimed in. She took a mouthful of the coffee she'd brought in from the staffroom. 'Just about everyone who's ever worked here at the hospital has accepted their invitations.'

'Fantastic!' someone else said.

Listening to the staff's enthusiasm about the coming weekend, Charge Nurse Liv Westerman felt her nerves shredding. She looked up from the notes she'd prepared for handover, pushing her dark hair back in a jerky movement. 'Sounds like it's going to be full-on fun,' she said lightly, hitching up a passable smile. 'Now, if anyone's interested in handover, I'd like to get out of the place, please?'

Instead of going home, Liv drove to her mother's neat weatherboard cottage, recognising her need for the familiarity of her childhood home and the reassuring quality of her mother's company.

A few minutes later, she popped her head through Mary Malloy's kitchen door and called, 'Hi, Mum. It's me.'

'Hello, love. Josh not with you?' Mary looked up from shaping some risen dough into several small loaves.

'He's got soccer training after school.' Automatically, Liv went across to the bench and switched on the electric kettle. 'I'll collect him about four-thirty. Cup of tea?'

'Lovely.'

While Liv got mugs down from the overhead cupboard, Mary slid the last bread tin into the oven. With her usual direct approach, she asked, 'Are you happy about this visit Adam's arranged, Olivia?'

'I suppose…' Liv hesitated, knowing *happy* was quite the wrong word for what she was feeling. She was scared witless about seeing her former husband again. For heaven's sake, it had been three years since they'd spent much time together.

Ever since Josh had been old enough to take the commuter flight to Sydney, Liv had encouraged him to spend time with his father. But now that Josh had turned twelve, he was often playing sport or doing something with his Scout troop on the weekend. He didn't *want* the interruption to his youthful activities to go and visit his father.

Liv shook her head, her clenched teeth beginning to ache. Her instincts were telling her Adam was getting fed up with their haphazard arrangement. And she agreed with him. The last thing she wanted was for Josh to become estranged from his father—the way Adam himself had been.

Liv stifled a sigh. She still felt guilty about the way their lives had turned out. For ages both before and after their divorce, she'd kept her hopes alive that she and Adam could sort out their differences and get back together.

But it had never happened. And whatever

should have been said or done between them had now been lost. For ever.

'The visit is really for Josh's sake, Mum.'

Mary looked keenly at her daughter. 'Well, that's good, isn't it? Josh is at a very impressionable age. I think it's wonderful Adam is taking leave to spend time with his son.'

Well, you would, Mum, Liv thought, but not unkindly. Her mother had always retained a soft spot for her former son-in-law.

'Where is he staying?' Mary asked now.

Liv watched as her mother warmed the pot and made the tea. 'At the Swagman's Inn.'

Mary tutted, slipping the blue and white tea-cosy over the pot. 'There was no need to spend good money on a motel. He could have stayed here with me.'

'You know Adam, Mum, he prefers his independence.'

'It's time he got over all that.' Mary clicked her tongue in faint disapproval. 'When is he arriving?'

'On Friday.' Liv's heart kicked and she swallowed. 'About midday, he thought...' The stark realisation sent twin curls of panic spiralling throughout her body, the past coming at her in a rush of images and scenarios containing so many *if onlys...*

Adam came from a very wealthy and powerful family. The Westermans had business interests everywhere in the state. But Adam had been a transient figure, away at boarding school, then later at university.

It had only been during vacation time that Liv and her friend Jacqui had caught an occasional glimpse of him as he'd sped along Bellreagh's main street in his high-powered sports car, black, like his mane of hair cutting through the wind behind him.

In the year they'd completed their higher education, Liv and Jacqui had decided to train as nurses at the local hospital. 'We'll be almost twenty-one when we've qualified,' Jacqui had said excitedly, 'and then we'll be able to travel. Being registered nurses means we'll have very portable jobs. We could go to Sydney or Melbourne or even overseas.'

'I suppose...' Liz had looked uncertain. 'I

mean, I really want to do nursing but I like living here. And there's Mum…'

Jacqui had snorted. 'Mary would be the last person to stand in your way.' She frowned a bit. 'Don't you want to travel, Liv?'

'Not as much as you, obviously,' Liv had responded wryly, and they'd both laughed and the subject had been dropped.

When they'd graduated, they'd combined to throw an informal party to celebrate their new status. Halfway through the evening, Jacqui remarked, 'We need to put more food out, Liv. Give me a hand, would you?'

Liv looked round at the rapidly depleting finger-food. 'Is it time for Mum's curry, do you think?'

'Terrific! Let's do it. Oh, my stars!' Jacqui hissed, a hand to her heart. 'Guess who's just walked in?'

Busy restoring the long trestle table to some kind of order, Liv answered absently, 'Who?'

'Tony Westerman!'

'Well, you said you'd invited him.'

'But I never thought he'd actually come! And, my God!' Jacqui's eyes were nearly popping out.

'Guess who's with him! Liv!' Her voice went into a muted shriek. 'They're coming over!'

Liv jerked her head up, her gaze riveted on Adam—tall, loose-limbed, wearing jeans and a casual knit shirt. She blinked, trying to imagine him in the white coat of a medical intern, and failed. This Adam Westerman looked more like a pirate, darkly handsome, wild and dangerous.

Tony greeted both young women with easy charm, adding, 'I don't think you've met my cousin, Adam.'

'Tony said it was all right if I came along.' Adam addressed Liv directly.

Liv blushed, watching the questioning frown notch into his forehead. His hands were folded across his chest, emphasising the hard strength of his forearms. Unaccountably and in wild confusion, she felt the urge to touch his skin, *stroke* the corded muscle. At the thought, she blushed more hotly and her words tumbled out. 'Yes—of course it is…'

And so it began.

They danced together for the remainder of the evening. And then, with his fingers laced firmly through hers, Adam walked Liv home, each too reluctant to speak lest they broke the spell of this strangely perfect evening.

Three months later, they were married.

Adam eased his foot back on the accelerator, flicking on the indicator and turning at the road sign marked BELLREAGH 20 KM.

The country was looking wonderful, he thought, lush and lime green, the farmhouses with their silver roofs baking in the afternoon sun. And everywhere he looked there were the wattle trees, their blossoms like golden powder puffs, marking the perimeters of paddocks and creek beds.

'Oh, boy,' he whispered, switching off the air-conditioning and opening the car's window. He took deep breaths, drawing the sharp smell of the eucalypts into his lungs and letting it soak in.

It was as different from Sydney as a place could be and he realised with something like wonder that there was now, as there always had been, a quaint unworldliness about Bellreagh…

'What the hell!' Adam jerked out of his

reverie, braking quickly as a young woman ran onto the road in front of him. She was bare-footed, her waist-length hair flying around her in a frenzy as she attempted to flag him down.

Adam's instincts shot into overdrive as *Emergency* flashed in neon lights across his brain. He brought the car to an abrupt halt, releasing the seat belt and throwing open the driver's door simultaneously.

As Adam's feet hit the road, the woman came to a stop beside him. 'Please… I need help…' Her breath was coming in painful gasps. 'It's my daughter—she's been bitten by a snake—'

'Where is she?' Adam's sharp tone snapped with authority. If the snake was of the venomous kind, there was no time to lose.

The young woman made a keening sound, gesturing to a cottage some distance off the road.

'Have you moved her?'

'I…told her to sit still.'

Adam felt a sliver of relief. They were buying time. He could only hope the child had obeyed her mother. Movement of any kind could speed up the passage of venom through the lymphatic system. And if the snake was a deadly red-bellied black or brown...

He exploded into a run.

Doing her best to keep up with him, the mother raised terror-filled eyes. 'Can you help her?'

'I'm a doctor. I'll do what I can. Have you phoned for an ambulance?'

'No phone.'

Adam swore explicitly under his breath, the burden of responsibility dropping heavily on his shoulders. He thrust the thought away and kept running.

It took only a few minutes to reach the cottage and another few seconds to locate the child in the back garden. She was sitting perfectly still on the grass, her arm with the bite propped against her hip and held away from her body.

Good little kid, Adam applauded silently, but she looked pale and shocked. Dropping beside her, he asked gently, 'What's your name, sweetheart?'

The child's mouth trembled. 'Emma...'

'Hello, Emma. I'm Adam. How old are you?'

'Ten. A snake bit me—here.' With trembling

fingers, the child pointed to where two ugly puncture marks were visible on the outside of her right palm just below her little finger.

Adam nodded, projecting calm. 'Did you see what kind it was?'

'A brown one.'

Adam's stomach clenched. The snake was one of Australia's most deadly. He shot upright and turned urgently to the child's mother. 'I'll need to bandage Emma's arm. Do you have an old sheet we could rip up?'

'Yes—I think so.' The mother ran.

And he'd need something he could utilise as splints. Adam's eyes were moving with lightning speed, coming to rest on an old-fashioned washing trolley against the side of the house. The thin wooden slats were weathered, almost white with age. He bounded across.

Turning the trolley on its side, he used his boot to kick the slats from their nailed position. They came away easily, separating cleanly from the main frame. Snatching up several for good measure, he sprinted back to the child.

'Will this do?' The mother came running

across the unmown grass, the sheet bundled in her outstretched arms.

Adam's head jerked up, for a fleeting second dwelling on the odd situation he'd landed in, but he felt a wave of sympathy for this mother. It was obvious she was doing her best under difficult circumstances.

He clamped his lips together. One quick look had told him the house was a falling-down dump, the yard overgrown—an obvious playground for snakes and God knew what vermin. And what on earth were they doing out here in the sticks without a phone?

Adam managed a reassuring nod. 'That's great, Mrs…?'

The mother gave him a tight, pinched look. 'Just call me Brittany.'

'Right.' Adam grabbed the threadbare sheet and began tearing it into strips. When he had enough for his purpose, he hunkered down again beside the child. 'Emma, I want you to hold your arm very, very still, just like you've been doing— OK? And, Brittany, I'll need you to hold the splints in place, after I bandage Emma's arm.'

'I can do that.' Brittany looked pathetically eager to help. Watching Adam pad up some of the linen and place a pressure bandage over the bitten area, she asked haltingly, 'Should I have washed the wound? I wasn't sure…'

'No,' Adam said immediately. 'That's not the way we treat snake bites any more. We do nothing but basic first aid, exactly as we're doing, until we can get Emma to hospital. They'll give her a shot of anti-venin to combat the snake's bite. OK, that should do it.' Swiftly and expertly, Adam tied off the makeshift bandage he'd wound from the child's fingertips right back to her armpit.

'Now, Brittany, move in closer. I want you to hold the splints in place while I immobilise Emma's arm. How are you feeling, sweet-heart?' he asked gently, and frowned. The child was looking glassily pale.

'A bit dizzy…' Emma drew air in through trembling lips. 'Will I be all right?' Blue eyes looked fearfully at Adam.

Adam felt his gut wrench. 'Yes, baby. You'll be fine,' he soothed, mentally crossing his fingers. Heaven knew how much venom the snake had injected. They needed to get the child to hospital—fast. He finished splinting. 'OK, let's go!'

Brittany gasped. 'I need to put some shoes on.'

'No time!' Adam tossed back over his shoulder, as he scooped the child up and began running. 'Come as you are!'

Adam belted his young patient into the passenger seat, deciding he could at least monitor her after a fashion on the way to the hospital. Grabbing a jumper he'd tossed there earlier, he tucked it around Emma and then ran round to the driver's side.

'Get in, Brittany—quickly!' He slammed the rear door after the young mother scrambled in and then leapt into the driver's seat himself. The Mercedes's engine started first time and within seconds they were travelling at top speed.

Very briefly, Adam had considered using his mobile to call for an ambulance to meet them and then just as quickly had rejected the idea. Even if an ambulance was available, it would take precious minutes to make the transfer—minutes they didn't have.

As they sped along the narrow bitumen road, Adam felt a swirl of mixed emotions well up like a balloon inside his chest. And it had nothing to do with the emergency he was bringing in. At this late stage, he'd begun doubting his decision to return to Bellreagh.

Just the prospect of seeing Liv again had his nerves hanging by a thread. Hell, where on earth had his confidence gone? He shouldn't be feeling this vulnerable.

With something like panic he saw the five-kilometre sign flash past. They were almost there and there was a knot in his stomach the size of a football. He just hoped Liv wasn't on duty in Casualty.

He wasn't nearly ready to meet her.

CHAPTER TWO

BUT today of all days, fate wasn't on Adam's side. Liv was the first person he saw when he ran into Reception.

'Adam…' His name came hoarsely from her throat.

'Emergency on the way here!' Adam snapped the words. 'Snake bite. This is Emma,' he said shortly, indicating the child in his arms.

'This way!' Liv's professionalism sprang into overdrive, all personal feelings swept aside. Quickly, she called to Suzy Barker, 'Page Dr McGregor, Suzy. He's needed in Resus.'

'Could we get her on oxygen, please?' Adam laid the child gently on the treatment couch.

Two minutes later Suzy popped her head in. 'Stuart is on an urgent consult. But I could haul out one of the residents—'

'No, it's all right.' Adam was tight-lipped. 'I'm a doctor. But could you look after Brittany here? She's Emma's mother.'

'Please—will she be all right?' Brittany cast a frantic look around the faces in the room.

'Your little girl will get very special care, Brittany.' Calmly, Suzy began removing the mother from the scene. 'Now, I'll need to get some details from you…'

Liv sent Adam a quick look. 'Looks like you're it, then.' For a second their eyes met, almost on a level, before she added hurriedly, 'I'll get the anti-venin.'

Her hands were shaking as she collected several ampoules from the drugs cabinet. I am *not* going to tie myself in knots about him being here, she vowed. Immediately, her breathing felt tight, mocking her resolution.

'Right. Let's have a listen, sweetheart.' Adam borrowed a stethoscope and flicked it over Emma's chest.

'Have we identified the snake?' Liv was back with the anti-venin.

'Emma said it was a brown.'

Liv nodded. 'They're prevalent at the moment. It's the mating season.'

His lip curled. '*We* should be so lucky.'

Liv felt her composure slipping every which way. What on earth was he playing at, making a loaded comment like that? As though there was some kind of easy rationale to explain the reasons they no longer had a marriage.

Adam's look intensified. 'I'd say she's around twenty-five kilos but we'll err on the side of caution and start with twenty mils.' He began to draw up the dose of anti-venin, his heart twisting. Poor little kid. What rotten luck for this to happen.

'I'll get a line in.' Liv's movements were quick and instinctive. They'd need to run normal saline to help flush out the poison from the child's system.

'I'd like Emma closely monitored, please,' Adam directed, as Liv secured the drip. 'We'll need to watch for any adverse reaction from the anti-venin.'

Liv kept her gaze averted. 'So, every five minutes for the first hour?'

'Please. We'll reassess after that.'

'In that case, we'd best hook her up to a Dynamap,' Liv suggested, mentioning the sphygmomanometer-like instrument that would automatically measure Emma's blood pressure. That way, the staff would be alerted immediately to any change. 'I'll just nip up and get one from CCU.'

'Bellreagh has a coronary care unit?' The drawled tone was little short of downright sarcastic.

Liv bridled. 'A tiny one but fully functional.'

'Excellent.' His response was mild. 'And bring a paediatric cuff, please.'

Liv took a thin breath. 'I'm well aware of the procedure, Adam. And this isn't some hick place either.'

'Did I say it was?'

'You implied it.' Liv shot out of Resus, her composure in pieces. Instead of taking the lift to the CCU, she pounded up the stairs, resentment in every line of her body. How on earth was she going to cope with this visit, when just a few minutes in his company had her so defensive and her nerves on fire?

* * *

'Great start, Westerman,' Adam muttered, grimacing with self-derision. The trouble was she'd thrown him for six all over again.

It had come at him in a rush, a heartbeat, the past coming forward and slipping into the present as if he were suddenly meeting the twenty-one-year-old Liv Malloy for the first time.

And in that instant he remembered everything from that first meeting, the way his gaze had spun over her face, registering every tiny detail from the tiny mole beside her mouth to the shining darkness of her hair and the cinnamon sprinkling of freckles across her nose.

But he'd never forgotten her eyes—although sometimes he'd wished he'd been able to. They were the colour of violets, drifting to an incredible shade of mauve when...

His gut wrenched. 'Get a grip!' he rasped under his breath. 'She's your *ex-wife*. Get that into your thick skull.'

So why on earth had he jumped all over her and acted so unprofessionally? Dammit, that crack about the hospital had been pathetic. Bellreagh was a great little hospital, always had been, with a dedicated permanent senior staff. And they were still attracting residents who were keen to get some rural medicine experience under their belts, when most rural hospitals were pushed just to keep their doors open.

Automatically, he checked Emma's pulse, trying to focus. But the past wouldn't be kept at bay...

He'd finished his internship here with Stuart McGregor as his mentor. Odd how the wheel turned round. Stuart, at that time, had been about his own age now—thirty-six.

After they'd got married, he'd stayed for Liv's sake. She hadn't wanted to move to Sydney. But once his internship had ended, he'd laid it on the line. He couldn't remain in the same town as his father. He had to get back to Sydney—to sanity.

And so, reluctantly, she'd given up her own job and everything she'd grown up with to go with him. And for a while he'd thought she'd managed the transition. But then Josh had been born.

And that had been when, despite their best efforts, their relationship had slowly, insidiously begun to falter…

Liv slipped back down to Casualty. Her thoughts were still in turmoil and Stuart had to call her twice before she looked up and saw him rapidly approaching.

'Sorry, I was held up.' He didn't break stride. 'Suzy said you had an emergency—snake bite. Patient still in Resus?'

'Stuart, it's OK!' Liv tugged him to a stop. 'She's been treated—by one of Sydney's top surgeons, no less.'

'I don't understand.'

She caught her lip. 'Adam's here.'

The senior registrar shook his head slowly, then lowered it and looked searchingly at her, realisation dawning. '*Your* Adam?'

Not any more. The truth sank through her, twisting and hurting but there were practical matters to be dealt with here. Stuart might be the kindest boss in the world but she couldn't let him go imagining Adam had come here for anything but to spend time with his son. 'We're divorced, Stu,' she reminded him quietly.

He gave an impatient snort. 'Silliest thing you ever did. You and Adam were made for each other.'

Liv put an anxious hand on his arm. 'Don't go saying stuff like that—especially to Adam. Please?'

The older man's eyes softened. 'Where is he?'

'In Resus with Emma. She's ten. I've just been to collect the Dynamap.'

'Good. I'll deliver it in person. Take a break, Liv.'

'Is that an order?'

'Yes.' Stuart didn't enlarge on it. 'I'm pulling rank, Sister. Now, scoot.'

'I'll arrange for someone to monitor the child,' she called to his rapidly departing back. The SR merely lifted a hand in acknowlededgment and kept walking.

For a second Liv hesitated, grateful for the breathing space Stuart had orchestrated. But that's all it was, she reflected. Sooner rather then later, she and Adam would have to sit down and talk.

'Ah, Liv.' Suzy shot out of one of the cubicles, clinging tightly to a kidney dish. 'Did Stuart find you?'

'Yes.' Liv snapped her thoughts together. 'But now I need someone to monitor Emma.'

'I'll organise it,' Suzy offered. 'Bianca's just back from lunch. This would be a good case for her to get involved in, don't you think?'

Liv nodded. Bianca was a relatively new RN whose experience was being widened by a stint in the A and E department. 'Thanks, Suz. Um…what have you done with Brittany?'

Suzy flapped a hand. 'I need a word about that. Can you hang on a tick?'

'I'll be at the nurses' station.'

Liv looked up sharply when the usually un-flappable Suzy almost fluttered into the station a few minutes later. 'Everything OK?'

For answer Suzy rolled her eyes and clasped her hands across her heart. 'He is *gorgeous*!'

Liv frowned. 'Who?'

'Your *ex*. I took Bianca down to Resus and Stuart introduced us. Why didn't you say something?'

'I've hardly had a chance.' Liv bit her lip. 'Adam's really here to see Josh, anyway.'

Suzy's muted 'Oh, *please!*' blew that assumption away before it could take hold. 'How long is he staying?'

'I'm not sure. *And* he's here a day early!' Liv's throat closed for a second and she swallowed unevenly. 'He was supposed to be arriving tomorrow...' And she'd expected a polite phone call when he arrived and time to compose herself before they met. Instead...

'You sound upset, Liv.' Suzy shot her friend a curious look. 'You've always given the impression you and Adam got on quite well.'

'On the *telephone,*' Liv clarified with feeling, the admission releasing a coiled painful tension inside her. 'Except for a very brief visit last year for his father's funeral, we hadn't been in the same room together for three years—until today.'

'Crikey,' Suzy breathed dramatically. 'So, it was all a bit fraught?'

'I really don't want to get into it, Suz.' Liv reached out to the fax machine, intercepting a report that had just come through. 'You were going to tell me about Brittany.'

'That's an odd business.' Suzy lowered her voice. 'She seems dead scared about something. Didn't even want to tell me her surname, until I assured her everything she told us would be treated confidentially.'

'Where is she now?' Liv asked.

'In the visitors' lounge. I raided the auxiliary committee's cupboard and managed to find her a pair of shoes and then asked Cait to get her a cup of tea and stay with her. She seems pretty desperate about the child, though. Blaming herself over Emma getting bitten.'

'Well, that's a fairly normal parental reaction.' Liv tried to keep her mind on the business in hand, but her gaze kept flicking back towards the resus area, as if expecting Adam to materialise any second.

'Maybe we should ask Robyn to have a word?' Suzy suggested, mentioning the hospital's social worker.

Instinctively, Liv held back. 'I think we should liaise with Stuart about that—and

Adam,' she added carefully, thinking that after all *he* possibly knew more about the woman's circumstances than any of them.

'You're probably right,' Suzy cheerfully agreed. 'Sad, though, that the old bogey about social workers is still prevalent. Even though most times they have the best of intentions.'

'Well, *we* know that. But if Brittany is as spooked as you say, the last thing we need is for her to feel she's being pursued by official-dom.' Liv managed a token smile and plucked her bag out from under the counter. 'I'll leave you to sort it, Suz. I'm off to the canteen for a coffee.'

'Aren't you going to wait for Adam?'

Liv felt her heartbeat accelerate to a rapid tango. 'I don't know how long he'll be...' she said awkwardly.

'So, go ask him.' Suzy motioned her head with its curly nimbus of red hair towards the resus area.

Liv opened her mouth and closed it.

'Sweetie, he's not going to bite you!'

Liv swallowed unevenly. Her head was in a spin and she was still fending off the sensual jolt of seeing her former husband again. 'If he asks, just tell him where I am.'

The canteen was set apart from the hospital at the end of a covered walkway. Liv entered through the electronic doors and looked about her.

It was past the normal lunch-hour but there were still small groups of hospital personnel scattered throughout the dining area. She gave a fractured sigh as she looked at the food on offer. Her stomach felt tied in knots and she doubted if she could swallow anything.

'Hello, Sister.' Meryl Jones, one of the canteen workers, trotted out from the preparation area. 'You're late today. But there's still some of the chicken fricassee left and a bit of rice, I think.'

Liv shook her head. 'Just a toasted cheese sandwich, thanks, Meryl. And a coffee—no, make that a pot of tea, please.'

'Right you are,' Meryl said cheerfully. 'Take a seat, love, and I'll bring it over.'

Liv nibbled on her sandwich a few minutes later, not really tasting it. If she was being honest, she had to admit it would be preferable if Adam found her here in neutral territory where they could perhaps begin to talk. But if he didn't show, did it mean her outburst earlier had put paid to him wanting to speak to her at all?

She sighed. When had it all got so complicated?

Deep in thought, she almost missed his arrival. Momentarily, she felt for the solidness of the chair beneath her, feeling as though, if she stood, her legs would collapse.

When he looked her way, she stiffened, her stomach lurching sideways. Their eyes tangled for a second before he flicked her a casual wave and made his way to the serving counter.

Watching him lean forward and exchange a few light-hearted words with Meryl, Liv felt her skin dissolve into goose-bumps. Her eyes flicked helplessly over him, faltered and went back for more.

His six-foot leanness was exactly as she remembered which probably meant he still ran every day to keep fit. His hair looked different from what she remembered. But the fashionably short cut suited him, transforming his handsomeness into something more mature. And—dare she even think it?—sexier.

She couldn't take her eyes off him. He was casually dressed in a white polo shirt and black chinos, making him appear more like the youthful Adam of their early days.

In a split second her body sprang to life, aching for him with a savage intensity that left her almost sick with its magnitude. 'Oh, Lord…' Her voice was a cracked whisper of breath. 'This can't be happening.'

By the time Adam had paid for his meal, scooped up his tray and made his way to her table, Liv had herself under control. Just.

'Hi.' He slid the tray on to the table. 'OK if I sit here?'

'Of course.' She saw he'd settled for the chicken fricassee and rice.

He picked up his fork. 'Mind if I dig in and save the chat for later? I had a pretty early start this morning.'

'Go ahead. Um, you're a day early.'

'Mmm. Got things squared away quicker than I anticipated. Thought I may as well make tracks to Bellreagh.'

Liv swallowed. 'H-how long are you staying?'

He gave a hard laugh. 'Want me out of the place already, Liv?'

'Not at all,' she said clearly.

His head came up and he blinked uncertainly. In her eyes he saw his own reflection and the misty mirror of their short marriage. His mouth tightened. 'Sorry for that, and about earlier,' he said gruffly. 'I acted like a clod.'

Liv fiddled with her cup. 'It's been a while, Adam. There was bound to be a bit of tension between us.'

One eyebrow rose. 'Perhaps. Just know I had no intention of playing the blame game. That came right out of left field.'

He went quietly on with his meal.

Liv stared through the window behind him, watching the tiny wagtails flick back and forth across the trelliswork and then dive low, looking for crumbs along the paving. Seeing him again was proving much harder than she'd imagined. And obviously for Adam as well, she had to admit. The realisation sanded the hard edges from her near-panic, allowing her to relax slightly.

'I thought I'd surprise Josh and pick him up after school.' Adam chased the last forkful of rice around his plate.

'Oh…' Liv looked pained. 'He's going to Scouts straight from school today. The troop leader usually drops them all home around six.'

Adam twitched a shoulder. 'That's fine.' But Liv could tell he was disappointed.

'Josh is off about his own business these days, Adam, spending time with his mates.' She tried to soften her remarks with a smile. 'Boring old home is the last place he wants to be sometimes. You know how it is.'

'No, I don't actually, Liv.' His voice held a trace of bitterness. 'I was packed off to boarding school when I was barely ten, remember?'

How could she have forgotten? Liv swallowed past the hard lump in her throat. After Adam's mother had died, that was exactly what had happened. Within weeks his father had remarried. His secretary, Julia, had become the second Mrs Westerman. And Adam had been sent away to school.

'Julia couldn't bear to have the child around,'

Mary had remarked once. Because little Adam looked so much like his mother…

'You'll have plenty of time to catch up,' Liv said, gently now.

'I'm counting on it. Our son is growing up fast, isn't he?'

'Yes.' She didn't enlarge on it.

'I guess we should start giving some thought to where he'll go for his high-school education.'

'That's not until next year,' she dismissed. 'Anyway, I imagine he'll want to continue on here.'

'He's starting to wonder about things, though. Last time he was with me in Sydney, he asked why we had to be divorced.'

Liv's stomach turned over. 'What did you tell him?'

'The truth—that we'd got married too young.'

'And was he satisfied with that?'

'Not really.' Adam leaned back in his chair, his loose-limbed frame oddly tense. 'With childlike logic our son commented, "Well, you're much older now."'

The words and their implication struck Liv as painfully as walking barefoot on broken glass. She caught the edge of her lip, meeting his gaze with difficulty. Did their son actually expect them to get back together? And not just their son. Did her former husband have an agenda here as well? The wild idea slammed into her brain with the impact of a lorry into a brick wall.

'For crying out loud, don't look like that, Liv.' His laugh was low and rough. 'If I'd thought there was any possibility of us reconciling, I'd have come back years ago.'

Liv looked away, staggered that he appeared to have given up so easily, when all along she'd tried to find a way through their problems in the hope of mending the rift between them. 'Despite *our* differences, I've made a good home for Josh,' she defended herself.

'I know,' he rejoined softly. 'What I said wasn't meant as a criticism. I'm just stating the way things are. How's Mary?' he sidetracked smoothly.

Liv gathered her shattered nerve ends

together, even managing the ghost of a smile. 'Mum's fine. Still working all kinds of hours.'

Adam's brows shot up. 'She's not still cleaning?'

'No, she's everyone's ironing lady these days. And I pay her for Josh's care, of course. But Mum *has* to work, Adam,' Liv said awkwardly. 'She's not old enough to qualify for a pension.'

'Why on earth haven't you said something, Liv? I could easily contribute to Mary's upkeep. Discreetly, of course,' he added with a dry grin.

Liv shook her head. 'She'd never go for that. She likes to be independent.'

'A trait she and I both share. I'll talk to her.'

'She won't listen,' Liv said firmly.

Their gazes locked for a moment and something flickered in his eyes. 'We'll see.'

Liv felt the nerves in her stomach coil. Why did she have the distinct impression he wasn't referring to her mother at all? Suddenly the silence between them felt loaded and dangerous. And in it she heard the door to the kind of intimacy she'd all but forgotten begin to slowly open...

Suddenly, she couldn't look at him, afraid of

what she'd see in his eyes—afraid of what he'd see in hers.

'Uh...how was Emma when you left her?'

Adam rocked his hand. 'Stabilising very slowly. But then we had to expect that. She'd displayed quite significant signs of envenomation.'

Which could lead to the worst possible scenario where Emma's blood would lose its ability to clot naturally. Imagining her own child in such a predicament, Liv suppressed a shudder. 'She'll need to remain in hospital for a few days, then?'

'Oh, yes, I'd say so.' Adam pursed his lips thoughtfully. 'If we could stretch things and allow Brittany to stay with Emma tonight, it would be helpful.'

'Shouldn't be a problem.' Liv hesitated and then asked carefully, 'Do you know anything about the family? It's just that Suzy said Brittany seemed reluctant to give out much— not even a surname.'

'I only know what I saw,' Adam said. 'The cottage where they're living is practically falling down.'

'Perhaps they're squatting.'

Adam shrugged. 'Perhaps. There was no phone, and one would have to wonder why Emma was not at school.'

'How would you feel about our social worker having a chat to Brittany?'

Adam's look sharpened. 'No—not yet. Let me see what I can do first.'

'Right.' Liv glanced at her watch. 'Oh, Lord, I should be back at work.'

'I'll walk with you.' Adam scooted his chair back and rose to his feet. 'Might be a good time to try and initiate a chat with Brittany.'

'Will you let me know how you get on?'

'Of course.' Adam's gaze met hers briefly and slid away. Damn, he cursed inwardly, feeling the strands of emotions knotting his gut, intermingling with the oddest kind of pain he couldn't account for.

CHAPTER THREE

'WAIT up, you two!' Stuart was bearing quickly down on them.

'Uh-oh.' Adam's dark brows edged together. 'I feel like an intern again, waiting to be hauled over the coals.'

Liv gave a choked laugh. 'He probably just wants a chat about Emma.'

But the SR didn't want to talk about their young patient at all. Instead, he folded his arms and eyed them squarely. 'I just wanted to tell you there's room for another couple at our table for the dinner-dance tomorrow night. You can make it, can't you?'

Adam and Liv looked helplessly at one another. And then Liv said bravely, 'I hadn't intended going, Stu.'

'Of course you must.' Stuart shook his fairishgrey head. 'Adam, I'm relying on you to buy the tickets and escort Liv. And I don't want to hear any excuses.' He held up his hands in a blocking motion. 'Every cent raised goes towards the hospital and we need all the help we can get.'

Adam's mouth twitched. 'It's not black tie, is it?'

'Well, if it is, no one's told me,' Stuart declared. 'Be a bit over the top for Bellreagh, don't you think?'

'Probably.' Adam stroked a hand across his chin, and sent a sharp look under his brows at Liv. 'OK with you?'

'We're being hijacked.' Her laugh was shaky and forced. 'But if Mum can have Josh over-night, then I guess it'll be all right.'

'Excellent. And we could do with another body on our tug-of-war team,' Stuart said, rubbing his hands, clearly on a roll. He sent a narrowed look at Adam. 'You look in good shape, laddie. Can I put your name down?'

Adam looked rueful. 'I guess so. Who are we pulling against?'

Stuart flapped a hand dismissively. 'Amateurs mostly.'

'Who are you calling *amateurs?*' Liv's tone held a laughing mock-rebuke. 'Our team's been training for weeks. We just might give you the fright of your lives.'

'Not likely.' The SR scoffed a laugh. 'I heard about your anchor-man crying off. Dicky knee, wasn't it?'

'Then, if that's the case, I think I should be on Liv's team.' With a sly wink at his former wife, Adam cranked up the banter. 'Families should stick together.'

'What a good idea.' Stuart looked smugly pleased. 'That should boost your team's chances, Liv.'

Liv managed a teeth-gritting smile. Clearly, she and Adam had been outmanoeuvred with style. And Stuart was looking as innocent as a newborn babe.

'I'll catch up with you later, folks,' he said, waving them on their way. Then he spun back to address Adam quietly, 'If you'd like to stick around and see Emma through this crisis, it's fine with me.'

'Thanks, mate.' Adam's mouth compressed for a second. 'I'd appreciate it.'

Liv looked at the time. Only a half-hour until the end of her shift. They'd been busy and she hadn't caught up with Adam again since their late lunch together. Settling herself at the nurses' station, she wondered if he'd managed to have a word with Brittany.

She worked automatically, collating her notes for handover, absorbed in her task.

'Any chance we could have a word?' Adam brushed her arm briefly across the high desk.

Liv's heart bounced wildly at the touch of skin on skin but she managed to say evenly, 'I'll just delegate someone to take handover and be right with you. Fancy a coffee?'

'Sounds good.' Adam scraped a hand across his cheekbones. 'Staffroom still in the same place?'

'More or less.' Liv nodded, regaining her equilibrium. 'It's been extended. These days we actually have a deck to relax on.' She sent him a trapped smile. 'See you out there in a few minutes.'

Adam had already got their coffees when Liv arrived. 'Still white with no sugar?' He pushed the steaming mug towards her.

'Mmm, thanks.' She huffed a jagged laugh. 'We always took our coffee the same way, didn't we?'

He gave a taut smile but refrained from answering.

Liv took a mouthful of her coffee and looked at him warily. 'So—any luck with Brittany?'

'There's an abusive boyfriend in the background apparently—not the child's father. Just someone Brittany unfortunately got hooked up with.'

'So, she's running scared?'

Adam's mouth pleated at the corners. 'Seems to be. She's scared he'll trace her if she goes to Social Security for help.'

'That won't happen,' Liv dismissed. 'She needs help, Adam—financial and every other kind, from what I hear. She must register with the social security office without delay.'

'She's scared stiff, Liv. Wild horses wouldn't drag her there.'

'But Mum might.' A smile nipped Liv's mouth. 'Mary is a registered hospital visitor, she often does stuff like this for patients and their families. She'll take Brittany under her wing.'

'I might have guessed.' Adam's look was wry. 'So, what should I do? Call Mary and explain we need a favour?'

'Or I will,' Liv offered.

'No, it's fine.' He shrugged off his ex-wife's offer. 'I'll do it. I was intending to call over and see her anyway. I'll collect Mary and bring her back here. And then I'll drive her and Brittany to the social security office.'

'I note you're not doubting Mum's powers of persuasion.' Her chin resting on her upturned hand, Liv flicked him a brief smile.

He sent her a guarded smile in return. 'Not for a minute.'

They finished their coffee quickly and in silence.

'I imagine the day hasn't turned out at all as you expected?' Liv said, with understatement as they made their way back to the A and E department.

'No,' he said abruptly. 'But I've quite enjoyed being part of the team, if only for a few hours. And it's been far better than kicking my heels in a motel room, waiting for you to finish work.' His gaze narrowed slightly. 'It hasn't been too much of a problem having me about the place, has it?'

'I—I suppose not.' Liv gave a strangled laugh, feeling the heat rising, warming her throat, flowering over her cheeks. Now that she thought about it, it hadn't been a problem at all.

In fact, she'd felt somehow warmed by her former husband's presence in the hospital. Which was odd, she considered now, given their less than harmonious beginning. 'You'll join Josh and me for dinner, won't you?'

'Well, it's more than I expected.' Adam's voice was carefully neutral. 'Seeing I've landed on you a day early. But, yes, thanks. I'd like that very much.'

Seeing the look of vulnerability in his eyes, Liv nibbled the edge of her bottom lip and frowned. Was he feeling so disenfranchised in his parental role he'd expected her to be inflexible about when he could spend time with their son? If he was, that was awful. Her heart thumped painfully and she felt a surge of regret for all the lost years.

'It looks like being a mild evening.' She pushed the words past the tight little knot in her throat. 'We'll cook something on the barbecue.'

'Can I bring anything?'

'Just yourself.' Liv hurried away.

Watching her walk towards the exit, Adam let his breath out in a slow stream of release.

God, it hurt just looking at her.

He blinked rapidly, his jaw tightening, and he felt again that edgy near-pain of desire. In a second the world he'd become used to, in a way had settled for, suddenly ripped apart and turned upside down.

Liv stopped by the supermarket on the way home. She'd rapidly reorganised the evening meal in her head, deciding the burgers she'd planned would not do. This evening called for something rather more special but something simple nevertheless. She didn't want to be labouring over a hot stove when Adam arrived.

In the deli she bought chicken fillets, decided she had the ingredients at home for a marinade and then picked up a bag of salad greens.

Her purchases made, she walked back to her car, her mind on the evening ahead. She had beer and white wine in the fridge but, knowing Adam, he'd probably bring wine anyway. They'd always enjoyed champagne when they'd been together but these days she never bought it. Too many memories.

Besides, it was a celebratory kind of wine and no fun drinking it on your own.

As she made her preparations for dinner, Liv realised she was wound up. Her mouth felt dry and her heart was skittering all over the place. What she wouldn't give for a normal family life—whatever that meant in today's sometimes mixed-up world. But she'd never planned to be a sole parent bringing up her son on her own.

Sighing inwardly, she took her mallet to the chicken fillets, flattening them out. Almost on autopilot, she prepared a marinade, blending the flavours of lime juice, honey and fresh ginger, adding a sprinkling of herbs she'd picked from the vegetable garden. Laying the fillets carefully in a flat dish, she spread the marinade over them. They should be delicious cooked on the barbecue later.

She washed her hands and then moved through to the lounge, carrying out a quick tidy-up. The big room with its warm maple floors and overstuffed sofas and the ancient pine dresser in the corner was just how she'd always wanted it.

Suddenly her hand went to her throat, memories as sharp as needles rising up to taunt her. Barely a year ago, she'd asked Adam whether he'd mind if she had the carpets removed and the floors restored to their natural wood-grain finish.

'Do what you like,' he'd said. 'It's your house.'

'Technically, it's yours,' she'd pointed out. 'You're paying the mortgage.'

'So what?' he'd snapped. 'You're my former

wife, not my tenant! Don't you think I want somewhere decent for you and our son to live?'

Her fingers tightened around the edge of the cushion she was holding and the sick feeling of trepidation was back again, tying knots in her tummy.

She sighed inwardly. She couldn't let the past colour this time Adam was going to be here with them. Already she'd sensed his need for family time and she was going to do all she could to make it happen. For all their sakes.

Filled with a new determination, she left the room and headed for the shower.

'You just off?' Stuart addressed Adam as they met in the hospital entry.

'Liv's invited me to dinner.' Adam was conscious of an absurd sense of light-heartedness and dangled his car keys impatiently. 'I'm about to grab a shower at the motel and head over there.'

'Good, good,' Stuart approved heartily. 'I won't keep you.'

'Emma's looking better.' Adam had taken a few steps but stopped and wheeled back. 'I'd

say she could go to the ward quite safely. Uh—
I'm assuming Bellreagh does have a kids' ward
by now.' He grinned disarmingly as he queried
the older man.

'Small but fully functional.' Stuart gave him
a dry look. 'I'll give you the tour some time. By
the way, did you manage to get those tickets for
the dinner-dance?'

'Yep.' Adam patted his back pocket. 'All paid
for.'

'Excellent. Ah—how long are you intending
to stay with us?' The SR leaned forward,
lowering his voice confidentially.

'I've arranged a week's leave.' Adam gave a
crooked smile. 'Mind you, with Josh at school
and Liv working, I guess I'll have a bit of time
on my hands.'

'I wonder…' Stuart stroked his chin. 'Perhaps
we could do one another a favour.'

'What do you need?'

Stuart's mouth flattened into a rueful smile.
'Couple of seminars in Canberra I wouldn't
mind attending.'

'When are they happening?'

'Middle of next week and the week after. Both sessions are geared to the needs of rural doctors and with a bit of luck, the health minister might be available for an informal chat.'

'So, an excellent chance to lodge your requests for more funding.'

'Something like that,' Stuart confirmed. 'If I could get to just one of them, it'd be a huge bonus. And I'd thought of taking an extra couple of days so Helen could come with me—' He broke off and scrubbed a hand around the back of his neck, looking sheepish. 'It's been ages since we've managed any quality time on our own.'

Adam gave a chuckle. 'How many kids is it now?'

'Five. And they're all fantastic. But, you know…' Stuart rocked his hand.

Not really. Adam felt the tightening in his throat again. He could only imagine what it felt like to have a real family. The fractured one he had now could hardly qualify. He managed a passable smile. 'So you'd like me to keep an eye on things here while you're away?'

Stuart looked hopeful. 'More or less be around

in a senior capacity. You'd see a lot more of Liv.'

Adam nodded slowly. 'There is that.' But would Liv want to see more of *him?*

'Look, Adam, don't feel pressured.' Stuart had seen the sudden tight set of the younger man's shoulders. 'The idea just occurred to me and I thought—'

'It sounds good.' Adam's dismissal was gruff. 'I'll do it. As I said, I've arranged cover for a week but I dare say that could be extended to two, even longer if you and Helen want to have a real break. Soak up the local scene. Canberra's nice at this time of year. You could do the wineries, take in a gallery or two. I seem to remember Helen's keen on the arts.'

'She is.' Stuart tugged both hands back through his hair and locked them at the back of his neck. 'You'd be doing me an enormous favour,' he added earnestly.

'On the contrary.' Adam grinned. 'I get to see more of my son, don't I? I want to do the very best for him, Stu.'

'Of course you do, laddie.' Stuart laid a gentle

hand on the younger man's shoulder and squeezed. 'But as a very wise person once said to me, "The best thing a man can do for his children is to love their mother."'

Perhaps she should have tried something a bit more adventurous than chicken, Liv fretted as she dressed hurriedly. At least made more of an effort for Adam's first meal with them in ages.

Lord, what did it matter anyway? Adam's whole purpose in coming this evening was to see their son. She had no doubt that he couldn't care less about what they ate.

Hastily, she pulled on a cotton skirt that swished around her calves, adding a top in a pretty aqua shade, its scooped neckline and little cap sleeves showing off her light tan. She took a steadying breath in and out. He'd be here any minute. She had just time to run a comb through her hair and swipe on some lipstick.

Adam realised the sick feeling of expectancy was back in his stomach as he brought the car to a stop outside Liv's house. And Stuart's parting words were still echoing in his head, confusing him, haunting him.

Should he have tried harder to hold their marriage together? But he'd tried as hard as he'd known how. They both had. But living in Sydney had been vastly more expensive and his salary at that time had barely met their overheads.

And his hours at the hospital had been cruel. When he'd got home, he'd only wanted to sleep. He'd been no company for his wife, had had no quality time to spend with their little boy.

He remembered the night Liv had tentatively suggested going back to work. 'I could try one of the private hospitals,' she'd said. 'Work day shifts only.'

'And what about our son?' he'd demanded. 'What are you intending to do with him while you work? Farm him out somewhere?'

'Don't be ridiculous, Adam. There are more than adequate childcare centres he could go to.'

'I don't want you going out to work!' he'd all but shouted.

'We need the money,' Liv had rounded on him. 'Everything costs twice as much here.'

Adam recalled the underlying panic in her voice. After a long time he'd said, 'I'll ask my father for a loan to tide us over.'

A blaze of hope had come into Liv's eyes and then faded. 'It's the last thing you want to do, isn't it?'

Adam had gone very still, all his energies reined in. 'I want you with Josh full time, Liv. He needs his mother. That's not too much to ask, is it?'

Adam took the key from the ignition, noticing the slight tremor in his hand. The rash journey back into the past had left him drained and uncertain. And why was he rehashing everything now? It was all too late. For the sake of their son, he and Liv had papered over the cracks and had a reasonable working relationship. Surely that was the best they could hope for?

Liv heard the doorbell with a sense of misgiving. Her hand went to her heart.

Taking a deep breath, she made her way along the hall and opened the door. Adam had his back to her, his gaze towards the street, his hands thrust deep in his pockets. He turned round smiling briefly at her. 'Hi. Not too early, am I?'

'Of course not.' She blinked. He was wearing cargo pants and a black sweatshirt that clung to the outline of his chest and shoulders, the sleeves pushed up his forearms. 'Come in,' she said, standing back out of the way.

He nodded. 'Thanks. Uh, I didn't bring any wine. I thought I'd wait to see what you're drinking these days.'

'I'm rather keen on the Rieslings.' Liv led the way through to the kitchen. 'But honestly, Adam, you didn't need to bring wine.'

'I know,' he countered, a small rueful twist to the smile he gave her. 'But I always used to…'

Liv swallowed dryly, fighting against the sudden intimacy that had sprung up between them. She began putting the salad together. 'There's beer in the fridge. Help yourself.'

Adam went to the fridge and selected a can of lager. 'Can I get you something?'

Liv shook her head. 'I'll have a glass of wine with dinner later.'

Adam relaxed against the benchtop, watching

as Liv quartered tomatoes and then sprinkled succulent black olives over the mixed salad leaves. He raised an eyebrow. 'Are we having a Greek salad?'

'Well, kind of,' she said tautly, all thumbs as he continued to watch her. 'I thought we'd grill some chicken on the barbecue to go with it— Oh, I just remembered!' She looked pained. 'You had chicken for lunch. We could do something else—'

'Liv, it's fine,' he said roughly. 'I don't give a damn what we eat.'

'I knew you'd feel like that…'

He laughed, a soft huff of sound that rippled over her nerve endings and made her insides go funny. She felt her heartbeat quicken. 'I think I might have that drink after all.'

She got down a glass from the cupboard and watched as Adam poured the wine. As he put the bottle back in the fridge, he straightened and asked, 'Would you mind if I had a look in Josh's room?'

She shook her head, slight surprise showing in the look she sent him over the rim of her glass. 'It's the last door on the right at the end of the hallway.'

Thoughtfully, Liv picked up a sponge to wipe down the benchtop. Adam had missed so much of his son's young life, she reflected sadly. The ordinary day-to-day happenings that formed the irreplaceable memories in a family.

Like the time Josh had flown his first kite, the gut-wrenching excitement when he'd won the under-eight sprint at the school sports, the tearful day when Jupiter, the black kitten, had been run over by the garbage truck...

Her expression was suddenly bleak. Adam had missed out on such a lot—probably half his son's life, in fact. She felt the tightness of tears in her eyes and hastily brushed them away.

A tiny pain began to gnaw away inside her as she remembered the time their marriage had seriously begun to unravel. They'd had a bitter argument and he'd vetoed her going back to work.

Now, older and wiser, she could see that Adam's insecurities as a child had been colouring his almost intractable stance. But then she'd seen his attitude only as little short of selfish.

Knowing of his uneasy relationship with his father, she'd been stunned when he'd suggested asking him for money. Wade Westerman hadn't approved of their marriage. Hadn't lifted a finger to help them.

'When will you ask him?' she'd said.

'This evening. I'll try to call to him during my dinner break—if I get one.'

Liv had been on tenterhooks and when Adam had rolled into bed beside her in the early hours of the morning, she'd woken in a flash. 'Did you manage to call your father?'

'Not now, Liv. I need to sleep.'

'It's all you ever do,' she said resentfully. 'I might as well be a log of wood—'

'All right!' Adam jackknifed from the pillow. 'I asked him. He set out his terms for a loan.'

Liv felt her throat go dry. 'And—?'

'I can't accept them.'

'But we have to, Adam,' she insisted, raising her voice. 'Why won't you take the money?'

He sank back heavily on to the pillow. 'I can't do it.'

Or won't do it. Liv was almost numb with

disbelief and anger. They lay in the darkness as far apart as possible to avoid inadvertent touching. The tension was stifling. Liv thought she might never sleep again and wished she could have moved into the spare bedroom—except they didn't have one...

Next morning when she'd dressed Josh and got his breakfast, they set out for the park. Exhaustion was eating into her limbs, her neck and her head ached. She couldn't live like this any longer. She'd make her own plans...

And we never really recovered from that awful time, she thought sadly now. The time when she'd packed up her own and Josh's belongings and come home to Bellreagh.

She'd tried explaining to Adam why she was leaving. 'You'll be freer without us. You can move back into the doctors' quarters. You'll have less pressure, less overheads. I'll get a job at Bellreagh Hospital and Mum will look after Josh.'

Adam's eyes had narrowed and grown flinty as she'd been speaking, and when she'd finished, he'd said tightly, 'And how are we supposed to keep this marriage going if you're so far away?'

Stung, Liv had rounded on him. 'If you'd accept this money from your father, I wouldn't *have* to go.'

'I can't accept it!' The sudden harshness in his tone had startled her.

'Then I'm leaving, Adam. It's the only way.' As soon as the words were uttered, Liv felt a sick rising panic. 'It won't be for ever—'

'Like hell it won't.' A nerve pulsed in Adam's tightly clenched jaw. 'Any excuse to get back to Bellreagh,' he accused. 'And don't even pretend you're doing this for *my* benefit.'

Liv hardly dared breathe. 'I'm doing it for all of us. Josh and I hardly see you anyway.'

'I can't help that.'

'I know. And I understand how consuming your work is just now.' She bent and picked up Joshua as he'd come trotting into the room. 'I'm just trying to find a way out.'

'By taking my son and running away.' Suddenly his face was wiped clean of expression. With deadly calm he said, 'I can see you've made up your mind. So go *home,* Olivia, if that's what you want. Go home and be happy.'

Now, she let her breath out slowly. There was no going back. Sadly, somewhere along the way, they'd made separate lives.

Lifting a hand, she pushed a wayward strand of hair away from her face, wondering whether she should join Adam in their son's bedroom or whether he wanted this time alone.

Finally, she steadied herself and made her way along the hall to Josh's room. She paused at the door and Adam looked up. He was seated on the edge of the bed, a large bound volume in his hand.

'This is rather advanced natural science,' he said, a faint frown marking his forehead. 'Does he actually comprehend the stuff?'

'He seems to.' Liv went into the room and dropped onto the bed beside Adam. 'Maybe our son is a budding naturalist.' Her teeth caught her bottom lip around a faltering smile. 'He wouldn't miss a TV documentary for anything.'

After an intense moment Adam shut the book with a snap and replaced it on the bedside table.

'I could have brought him a video along those lines. But the fact is, I had no idea what to get him.' His jaw tightened. 'Pathetic, isn't it?'

'Adam, don't beat up on yourself. Josh loves you—not the presents you give him.'

He stared broodingly at her. 'I don't see him enough.'

Liv's heart began beating rapidly. 'Are you blaming me?'

He made a dismissive sound in his throat, shooting to his feet and taking her with him. Still holding her wrist, he dipped his dark head to look at her. 'I'm not blaming you. But we've made a mess of things, haven't we, Livvy?'

She swallowed thickly, his pet name for her almost undoing her composure. She licked her lips. 'We can't go back, Adam.'

'Let's not, then…' He touched his knuckles to her cheek, a touch so gentle, so unexpected she felt her knees go to water. It took every last gram of her willpower to resist the urge to incline her head towards his touch, to prolong it. To extend it into something else entirely.

What might have happened, she didn't know.

Suddenly, the sound of a car door slamming had them both turning.

'Sounds like our boy's home,' Adam observed with a strained smile.

'He's going to get a surprise when he sees you.'

'Good.' Adam began to guide her towards the door. 'I can't wait to see him.'

'Mum?' Josh made his way into the kitchen, hurling his backpack onto the end of the benchtop. He turned, his dark head at an enquiring angle. 'Who owns the wheels out front—? Dad!'

'Hey, mate.' Palm up, Adam stepped forward, offering his son a high-five greeting. 'I'm here a day early,' he said, ruffling the boy's hair.

'Cool. How long have you had the Merc?'

'A few months.' Adam's mouth folded in on a smile. 'I must have forgotten to tell you. Haven't seen you for a while.'

'I've had stuff on…' The boy looked uncertainly at his mother.

'Dad understands, love,' Liv said, and hoped to heaven Adam did. 'Shoot off into the shower now. Dinner won't be long.'

Josh perked up. 'What're we having?'

'We're doing chicken on the barbecue.'

'Cool! And chips?'

'In your dreams.' Liv smiled. 'We're having salad.'

'He's grown so much,' Adam's gaze was wistful as he watched the boy race off.

Liv nodded. 'He's almost grown out of his clothes again. It's good you came, Adam.' She looked up at him. One part of her, the sensible part, was telling her she didn't want to be standing here, this close to him. She could see the hazel flecks in his dark eyes, see the way his hair had fallen across his forehead.

She had an almost desperate need to stroke it away, like she once had. She wanted to reach up and touch his face and for him wrap his arms around her and tell her everything was going to be all right—that they could start again…

Adam stared down at her, losing himself, and for a second anything was possible. His heart did a back flip in his chest. Mentally, he backed away. He was imagining things. 'We, uh, should get the barbecue under way,' he said, suddenly short of breath.

'Yes—fine.' Liv spun round, groping blindly for the support of the benchtop. Something had flickered in his gaze. Something she couldn't clearly define. Her throat felt thick as she swallowed. 'Let's do that.'

CHAPTER FOUR

'GREAT food, Liv. Thanks.'

She lifted a shoulder modestly. They were on their own, Josh having excused himself to explore the new computer game his father had brought him. 'It was pretty ordinary, really.'

'From where I'm sitting, any home-cooked meal is far from ordinary,' Adam countered dryly.

'Do you cook much these days?'

His mouth turned down. 'Now and again. I can manage a reasonably decent omelette and shove a steak under the grill, potatoes in their jackets—that kind of thing.'

'Perhaps you should leave the cooking to your girlfriends.' Head bent, Liv gave an off-key little laugh, as she stood to her feet and began clearing the table after their informal meal.

'That's hardly politically correct these days.

Anyhow, I don't have any girlfriends I could ask to cook for me.'

'That's odd.'

'What is?' he shot back, his dark brows furrowing.

'That you don't have a girlfriend.'

'Why is it *odd?*' He was scanning her face, waiting for her reply.

Liv coloured faintly. 'I don't know. You're single again. I just assumed—'

'Do *you* have a boyfriend?' he cut in smoothly.

She took a sharp breath, the tray of dishes clutched to her chest. 'No.'

He gave the flicker of a smile. 'So that's cleared that up, hasn't it?' Standing, he leaned across and took the tray from her unprotesting hands and proceeded to make his way back inside.

Liv gathered the placemats they'd used and followed him. She watched as he carefully stacked crockery and glasses in the dishwasher. 'Coffee?'

'Sounds good.' Adam closed the door on the dishwasher and straightened. 'I'll make it. Do you have the real stuff?'

'Yes.' Liv fussed around, showing him where everything was. Her thoughts began flying every which way. It felt strange, to say the least, to have a man in her kitchen again.

Especially when that man was her former husband.

She arranged some tiny pieces of shortbread on a plate and added it to the tray. 'I'll—uh—just see if Josh wants a glass of milk or something,' she said quickly.

When she returned, Adam had made the coffee and had parked himself against the benchtop, arms folded, feet crossed at the ankles. He raised a brow in query.

'No, he's fine.' Liv lifted a hand, her fingers pleating the neckline of her top. 'Rapt in his new game.'

'So, what do you say we take the coffee through to the lounge and make ourselves comfortable?'

His smile left a lingering warmth in his eyes and Liv felt her heart lurch.

Adam placed the tray on the cedar chest in front of the sofa and then guided Liv down to sit beside him. 'How late will you let Josh stay up?' he asked.

'Not for much longer.' She leaned forward and sent the plunger down on the coffee. 'He's usually pretty good about bedtime on school nights. And he runs himself ragged on the weekends so he's off to bed early then as well. He's basically a good kid, don't you think?'

'Mmm.' Adam hunched forward, his hands linked between his knees. 'He can pack the food away, certainly.'

Liv chuckled and handed Adam his coffee. 'He's a growing boy.'

'I'll arrange to have more money put into your bank account.'

'That's not necessary, Adam.'

A frown flickered in his eyes. 'You've mentioned he's outgrown his clothes and I can only imagine your food bill. Besides, how else can I take care of you?'

His question hung in the air like a precipitate clap of thunder. 'You're more than generous now.' Liv searched carefully for the right words.

'You've provided us with this lovely house and—'

'I need to be more of a hands-on father,' he cut in deliberately.

She took a controlling breath, her nerve ends quivering with tension. 'OK. I'll make changes. Ensure Josh gets to see you more often—as often as you like.'

'I need more than that, Olivia.' His dark eyes homed in on her, their brilliance nearly blinding her.

'Like what?' Liv felt her mouth go stiff.

He huffed a bitter laugh. 'I don't know yet. I just know from my point of view, the present state of play is lousy.' Finishing his coffee quickly, he got to his feet. 'I'll just say good-night to Josh and be on my way. I want to swing by the hospital and check on Emma before I head back to the motel.'

Liv lay wide awake, staring at the ceiling. *I need more than that.* Adam's words had been going round and round in her head since he'd left.

And the whole essence of him was still in the house. Haunting her.

What did he mean by *more?* And *hands-on* was another phrase he'd used. What did it all add up to? Suddenly, a chill of fear ran through her and her heart began to pump wildly.

Was he about to demand a change in their custody arrangements?

She finally slept, rising early as usual, and under the needling warmth of the shower dragged herself together, at least enough to face another day.

But the dregs of unease were still with her. As she dressed for work, she wondered on what grounds Adam could pursue custody. Their son was happy and well adjusted. All his teachers said so. And it wasn't as though she left him to fend for himself at any time.

When she worked an early shift, as she'd done all this week, she dropped him at her mother's. Mary gave him breakfast and saw him safely onto the school bus. But now and then, like all children, Josh had days when he was off-colour. And at those times Mary would come and stay

with him so Liv could go to work in the knowledge that Josh was being well looked after.

Her fingers were quick and skilful as she
twisted her hair into a loose knot for work. Adam
could never claim she was an unfit mother.

Never.

She'd have it out with him today, she decided
grimly. He was bound to show up at the
hospital some time.

When she came on duty, her nerves were
strung tight. She took handover and wondered
where on earth the rest of the team for the early
shift had suddenly disappeared to.

Stifling a sigh, she consulted the night sister's
report. By the look of things, she'd be hard-
pressed getting any sense out of folk with the
whole place hyped-up over the wretched
dinner-dance this evening.

That thought brought another river of unease
flooding over her. Perhaps by this evening she
and Adam wouldn't be on speaking terms, let
alone on dancing terms. *Dancing?* The mental
picture of Adam holding her close had another
rush of uncertainty claiming her.

Get a grip, she admonished herself silently. It'll be all right. We'll be amongst friends—curious friends, a little imp of mischief reminded her. So? She gave a dismissive lift of her shoulder. They'd eat, dance a little, or maybe they wouldn't dance at all...

'Excuse me, Liv?' Cait, the young nursing assistant leant over the high counter of the station. Gaining Liv's attention, she said quietly, 'That old guy is back again. What should I do with him?'

'You mean Vinnie? Old chap with a beard?'

Cait nodded. 'Bianca said he only comes in for a chat and a cup of tea, so should I shoo him off?'

'No, don't do that.' Liv swung down from the high swivel chair. 'The one time you might see him off could be the time he's actually ill. Anyway, we always get him a cup of tea, don't we?'

'I think so.' Cait looked uncertain. 'So, I'll do that, shall I?'

'No, I'll have a chat to him first.' Liv glanced at the time. 'Have you seen the rest of the team, Cait?'

'Uh…' The youngster bit her lip. 'In the staffroom, I think.'

'Still?' Liv's brows shot up, her mouth set. It was shaping up to be one of those days! She hated having to pull colleagues into line, especially when they all should know better than to be trickling into the department when it suited them. Resolutely, she began to walk towards the casualty area.

'Good morning, Vinnie.' Liv dropped into a chair beside the elderly man. 'How can we help you today?'

Vinnie wheezed a bit. 'Wouldn't mind a cuppa, love.'

'Well, that can be arranged.' She smiled, lifting his wrist and looking down at her watch to check his pulse. She made a little moue of concern. 'Are you not feeling well?'

'Feeling a bit weak, chest hurts when I breathe, like…' He tapered off and coughed into a hanky.

'Right.' Liv made a snap decision. 'Let's get a doctor to have a look at you, shall we? Cait here will take you along to the examination room.'

Where is a doctor when you need one? Liv cast a slightly exasperated look up and down the emergency department. Stuart wasn't on duty until later but their resident, Luci Chalmers, should have shown her face by now.

'Can I help?'

Liv spun round. The tone of Adam's voice clearly indicated he'd picked up on her frustration.

To cover her confusion, she bit out irritably, 'This place is a shambles this morning. You're in early,' she tacked on almost accusingly.

'I've been for a run and had breakfast,' he said calmly. 'I thought I'd wander in and say good morning.'

Liv was taken aback. She rolled her bottom lip between her teeth. 'Then good morning to you as well.'

'You might look as though you mean it.' His remark was touched with dry humour. 'Did you get out of bed grumpy?'

What if she had? Beds and how she got out of them were none of his business. Not any more. Liv brought her chin up. Her thoughts were churning and she snapped back into her professional role, as if her life depended on it. 'Would you mind taking a look at a patient?'

'Not at all.' He narrowed a glance at her. 'Fill me in.'

'Vincent Bourke, seventies, a regular in Casualty, wanders in for a chat, the odd small ailment. We usually give him a bit of attention, a hot drink and send him off.'

'Every casualty department has its share of eccentric customers,' Adam responded smoothly. 'So, what's different about your Vincent today?'

Liv raised a shoulder. 'Just a niggling feeling I have. I think he may be brewing something. But, then, maybe I'm wasting your time…'

'You're not wasting my time, Liv. Trust your instincts. I know I do.'

Their eyes met for an intense moment before each looked away uncertainly.

'Vinnie's in exam room one.' Liv began to lead the way. 'Do you want a white coat?'

He snorted. 'Except for consults, I practically live in scrubs when I'm on duty. As far as I'm concerned, white coats should have gone out with niddy noddies.'

'Sorry?'

'Small wooden contraptions,' he explained. 'Used centuries ago for holding wool while you wound it. Mary told me about them once, when she was knitting me a jumper.'

Liv's heart kicked and she swallowed. This was an insane conversation. 'Bulky knit in navy, wasn't it?'

'You remember.'

She turned her head and looked at him. They shared a ragged smile, his lopsided and faintly strained.

'I wore it for ages.'

Liv felt her composure slip. And she realised her panic that her former husband had some kind of secret agenda suddenly seemed ridiculous. He wouldn't do that to her. 'In here,' she croaked, and led him into the cubicle, standing rather protectively beside Vinnie.

Adam was thorough. And she felt a rush of gratitude that he'd taken her concern for this nice old man on board.

Slowly and carefully, Adam began palpating his patient's stomach. Liv knew he'd be checking for any hardening that could indicate a serious problem with one or more of Vincent's internal organs.

Gently, she brought Vinnie into a sitting position and handed Adam a stethoscope.

'Thanks,' he murmured. 'I'm going to have a listen to your lungs now, Vincent, so will you cough for me, please? And again. You've a few rattles in there. How long have you been feeling ill?'

'Couple of days…' Vinnie wheezed. 'Felt real crook when I woke this morning…'

Adam nodded. 'It's good you came in to see us, then. We'll arrange some treatment for you.' He went across to the basin to wash his hands, drying them quickly. 'I'd like a word now, please, Olivia.'

They stepped outside the cubicle and Liv pulled the curtains closed. She looked questioningly at Adam.

'He's exhibiting early signs of pneumonia.' Adam frowned. 'And he's quite seriously dehydrated.'

'So you'll admit him.'

'I'd like to. What's our bed situation?'

'Several available for allocation. I've just checked.'

'Good.' Adam pulled out his pen and took the chart Liv handed to him. 'I'd like Vincent X-rayed for starters, both bases of lungs. And a sample of sputum, please, Liv. We'll see what that tells us.'

'I'll see to it personally.' It was probably the only way anything was going to get done today, she reflected ruefully.

'The sputum culture may take a while,' Adam said consideringly. 'So, in the meantime, we'll start Vincent on a drugs regime. We may need to change it slightly when we get the lab results.'

Concern was etched on Liv's face. 'Vinnie's a great old boy. He will be all right, won't he, Adam?'

'I should think so.' He began making a notation of the drugs he wanted used. 'We'll start with Amoxil four-hourly and benzyl six-hourly, both delivered IV.' He clicked his pen shut and slid it back into his shirt pocket. 'Normal saline to get his fluids back up as a priority.'

'Right. Thank you for all that.' Liv sent him a contained little smile. 'We'll have to put you on the payroll.'

Adam opened his mouth to tell her he was about to be, but changed his mind. He'd tell her later when they had a moment to themselves. 'Ah…' He lifted a hand and rubbed the back of his neck. 'When you have Vincent settled in the ward, page me and I'll come up.'

'You want to stay as the treating doctor?'

'Please. I'll clear it with Stuart. I'm sure it won't be a problem.'

Liv's mouth went up in a wry little twist. 'That's a whole two patients you've acquired already.'

'Yep.' With a mere lifting of his hand, Adam took off. After a few steps, he turned. Without slowing his stride, he skipped backwards and called, 'Well spotted, by the way.'

Liv watched his long-limbed stride as he walked off. He'd slotted into the place so easily, as if he'd never been away. She swallowed a sliver of unease.

What *had* she expected from Adam's visit? She didn't know. Hadn't let herself think too deeply about it. But surely he didn't need to be hanging about the hospital so early, did he?

Thank God he'd be gone again in a few days. Absolutely the last thing she needed was an ex-husband underfoot, playing havoc with her feelings.

With quiet efficiency, Liv got the shift under way, delegating Vinnie's care to Suzy. Suddenly, for reasons she didn't care to analyse, she wanted to stay out of Adam's orbit.

The morning began to hot up. Several walking wounded had already arrived. In one of the cubicles Liv found a youngster not much older than her own son and obviously alone. He was sitting on the treatment couch, his feet dangling over the side. Her gaze dropped to the piece of rag around the boy's foot. 'Hi.' She smiled. 'I'm Liv. Has anyone been in to see you yet?'

The boy shook his head. 'The nurse just told me to wait.'

Liv looked at the chart in the rack and saw the boy's name was Nathan Banks. 'So, Nathan...'

She turned away, pulling on gloves and bending to dispense with the makeshift bandage. 'Mum or Dad not with you?'

'Dad took off last year,' the boy said with scorn. 'Mum works at the cannery.'

Liv inspected the boy's injured foot. 'How did this happen?'

'Cut it when I was delivering papers this morning. Stood on a broken bottle. I didn't see it in the grass.'

'You weren't wearing shoes, I take it?'

Nathan merely shrugged.

The cut was dirty and would certainly need stitching. Liv stripped off her gloves. 'How did you get here, Nate?'

'Mr Evans from the paper shop dropped me off.' The boy chewed his lip. 'He reckoned I'd need stitches.'

'You will, but I promise you won't feel a thing. Now, we'll have to contact your mum. We'll need her to sign for your treatment.'

'She's not allowed phone calls at work.'

'I'm sure her boss won't mind once he knows it's an emergency.'

Nathan looked stricken. 'She'll get in trouble—'

'No, *we'll* get in trouble if we go ahead and treat you without her consent.' Liv was gentle but firm. 'Is there another relative we could contact perhaps? A gran or granddad? Auntie?'

Nathan hesitated, staring down at his hands. 'It's just Mum and me.'

'It'll be OK, honey.' Liv gave his shoulder a little reassuring pat. 'We'll sort something out.'

She left the cubicle, her shoulders lifting in a dispirited sigh. Here was yet another family without a resident father. She thought of Brittany and Emma soldiering on alone and then for good measure added herself and Joshua to the trio.

Was it a sign of the times they lived in? she wondered.

'Oh, Liv!' Bianca hailed her from the station. 'I was looking for you.'

'You see me.' Liv made her way in behind the high counter. 'What's up?'

'Nathan—young kid with the cut foot? I called his mother's workplace and asked to speak to her. I couldn't get past the reception-ist. She gave me a flat "Employees aren't allowed personal calls."'

'What century are these people living in?' Liv stormed.

As if it wasn't difficult enough being a sole parent, without these kinds of moron bosses to contend with as well. 'Do you have the number, Bianca? I'll sort this out.' Or lose my own job trying, she added grimly, snapping up the cordless phone and punching out the number the other nurse had written down.

Several minutes later, Liv dropped the receiver back on its cradle. 'Stupid man.'

She looked up and half turned to find Adam standing there, his mouth twitching. 'Which one?' he asked cheerfully.

'The boss at the cannery!' Liv blew out a frac-tured sigh and tipped her gaze heavenwards. 'I was trying to get the message into his thick head that the child of one of his female employees is here in Casualty and we need her for a signature.'

'Surely he didn't object to her taking time off?'

'Not after I'd explained things for the umpteenth time. When the penny finally dropped he offered to drive Mrs Banks here himself.'

'There you are, then.' Adam's smile unfolded lazily. 'Shows what a good piece of facilitating you've achieved.'

'With no help from the so-called manager,' she scolded. 'By the sound of him, I think he'd feel more at home swinging from tree to tree in the jungle.'

Adam's lips took on a slightly wry curve. 'Want me to hide the bananas, then, before he gets here?'

Her mouth kicked up in an involuntary smile. 'We're not being very charitable, are we?'

Adam merely lifted a shoulder dismissively. 'Do you need me to look at your patient?'

'It's fine, thanks,' she said hurriedly, wanting to put some space between them. 'I'll have a word with our resident. She and Bianca can sort out the patient and the paperwork between them.'

'So, can you free up a few minutes to join me for a coffee?'

She blinked uncertainly. Lord, it was still there, this wild kind of sexual energy that had been humming between them since he'd arrived. 'I—uh—suppose I could. Are you just back from the ward?' she tacked on, covering her confusion by flicking up a stray stethoscope from the back of a chair and then shoving it on top of some computer printouts.

'Mmm.' Adam parked himself against the corner of the desk. 'Vincent is all settled in.'

'And Emma?'

'Doing well.'

'Any joy about rehousing the family?'

'Good result there. Stuart's a big wheel in the Rotary Club. He's managed to call in a few favours and get a furnished cottage in town made available. Brittany can move in as soon as she likes.'

'That's great,' Liv approved softly. 'And so like Stu.'

'Yes, it is.' Adam pushed himself upright. 'Could we go now, before you get caught up again?'

Liv flushed. 'I'll just have a word with Bianca. Meet you in the canteen?'

His mouth curved into a crooked moue and he

shot her a hopeful glance. 'I thought we could go across to my motel. The restaurant's open for breakfast. Coffee should be still on. But even if it's not, I'm a guest so they'll look after us.'

Liv looked wary.

'It's only a few minutes away,' he cajoled softly. 'And I need to discuss something with you, preferably away from the hospital.'

Something? What kind of *something?* Liv felt as though a whole colony of butterflies had suddenly taken up residence in her stomach. Was it about custody arrangements? But surely he wouldn't spring it on her like this—over a quick cup of coffee?

She moistened her lips. 'All right. Just let me organise a couple of things.'

'Meet you outside. We'll go in my car.' Adam looked into her eyes and saw a flicker of alarm. He made a muted sound of disgust in his throat. 'Give me a break, Liv.'

She shot him a startled glance and was shaken by the almost hurt expression on his face. She bit down on her bottom lip. 'It…just feels *odd,* having you about the place.'

'We'll go in separate cars, then, if it will make things easier for you.'

Liv sent him a trapped smile. 'That's silly.' The words came out low and husky. 'I'll meet you in the car park.'

'I feel a bit conspicuous in my nurse's uniform,' Liv commented a few minutes later, as they made their way into the motel restaurant.

Adam flicked her a glance and his cheek momentarily creased. 'As long as you're not covered in blood, I doubt anyone will notice.'

Liv made a face at him and slid into the chair he held for her.

'Would you like something to eat with the coffee?' he asked politely.

Liv felt her tummy rumble as though it was answering his question. And she would like something, she realised. She'd been too stirred up to eat much breakfast. 'If they do raisin toast, I'll have some of that, thanks.'

Adam nodded. 'I'll go and see if I can rustle up someone. Looks like breakfast is finished.'

Liv looked around her. The restaurant was in

a pleasant setting, with lattice doors leading out onto a terrace. Already the sprinkler hose was playing gently over the shrubs and potted plants that edged the perimeter.

It was Bellreagh's most upmarket motel but she'd never been here to the restaurant. Strange, that. Or possibly not so strange. It wasn't the kind of place she'd come to with Josh or Mary. And she hadn't dated anyone in a long time…

'OK?' Adam let his hand rest briefly on her shoulder, before swinging into the chair opposite.

'Yes, fine,' Liv said quickly, pushing her wayward thoughts into shutdown. 'What did you want to talk about?'

He looked at her rather broodingly, his brown eyes darker than usual. 'You really don't want to be here with me at all, do you, Liv?'

'It's not that.'

'What, then?' he inquired softly.

Her heart thudded painfully. She couldn't tell him she was afraid he was about to turn her safe, predictable life upside down. 'Why don't you just tell me what's on your mind, Adam?'

A significant silence. And through it, the waiter brought their coffee and raisin toast.

'Thanks,' Adam said gruffly. When the waiter had gone, he leant over and took her left hand. 'I only wanted to tell you my plans have changed slightly.' His thumb began smoothing absently over her knuckles. 'Stu wants to attend a conference in Canberra, take Helen with him and tack on a bit of a holiday. He asked me if I could cover for him and I've agreed.'

'How long will he be away?' she asked stiltedly, more than a little unnerved by the arousing effect his stroking was having on her senses.

'Couple of weeks. Maybe a bit longer.' Adam released her hand abruptly. Lifting the coffeepot, he began to pour.

Liv felt almost sick with vulnerability. 'You didn't think to discuss it with me before you agreed?'

He frowned. 'I thought you'd be happy for me to have more time with our son. Hell…' His mouth tightened fractionally. 'Surely you don't begrudge me that, Olivia?'

Of course she didn't. Not if that was *all* he wanted. But how could she be sure he didn't have another agenda entirely?

Like what? the sane sensible part of her brain admonished. But these days her former husband was rich and powerful.

And he'd never forgiven her for taking their son and leaving their marriage. Even if she'd meant it to be only temporary.

Lord. She forced herself to take a huge steadying breath. She had to stop thinking these negative thoughts and start building bridges or the next two weeks would be unbearable. 'Sorry.' She took the little jug and poured milk into their coffee. 'I'm glad you're having more time with Josh. He'll be over the moon.'

But not *you.* Adam didn't trust himself to look at his former wife. Everything was proving far more difficult than he'd imagined. But he needed Liv on side if they were to achieve anything worthwhile from his visit.

He'd have to curb his impatience, watch where he put his size nines, he thought resignedly. Nothing would be resolved if he stormed all over her—not that he wanted to. But, sweet heaven, couldn't she meet him halfway?

'So, are you looking forward to the dinner-dance?' Liv's question was deliberately light and accompanied by an over-bright smile.

Adam laughed a bit hollowly. 'I can't see us getting out of it, can you?'

Did he want to? Her unease climbed another few notches. 'We needn't stay long…'

Adam took a deep breath and let it go. 'It'll be fine.' He flicked her a rueful smile. 'Who knows? We might even enjoy ourselves.' He picked up his coffee and took a slow mouthful.

'Is it OK with Mary to have Josh for the night?' Adam asked the question as they made their way back along the tree-lined walkway to his car. As if by mutual consent, they'd managed to keep the conversation on neutral ground while they'd finished their coffee.

Liv nodded. 'She loves having him.'

'I guess he spends quite a bit of time there—with your work schedule and so on.'

Was he objecting? Finding fault with her care

arrangements for their son? Liv felt her pulse jerk. 'Are you saying he shouldn't be spending so much time with his grandmother?' she snapped.

'No, I'm not.' Adam's mouth compressed, his annoyance almost tangible. 'What's with you, Olivia? Last night you told me it was good that I'd come to spend time with Josh. This morning you're spoiling for a fight about it. I've tried to tread gently but I have rights, too. Don't try and take them from me.'

'I wouldn't! I'd never do that!'

'Then tell me what's got you so downright defensive around me?' he demanded, catching her arm as she'd begun to stalk off and bringing her round to face him.

Her head snapped up, her eyes meeting his, awareness of his strength and dark masculinity sending her senses spinning.

Suddenly, wildly, the atmosphere was charged with danger. For one brief shattering moment Adam's glittering gaze burned into her.

Liv could hear the pulse of her blood pounding in her ears. She made a tiny sound in her throat. Her eyes, wide and startled, met his and her lips parted a fraction.

It was too much for Adam. His throat worked as he rasped her name, drawing her into his arms and lowering his mouth to hers. Her lips tasted like nectar, so soft, so giving, involuntarily parting to allow him access.

A violent shiver ran through him as her arms crept around him. Tightened. The slow-burning heat he'd struggled to contain from the moment he'd set eyes on her yesterday raged out of control, the feel of her ripe warm body pressed against his, almost sending him over the edge.

Livvy. He wanted her, needed her in a way he'd forgotten he could need, and only the dark reminder that she was no longer his wife stopped him from scooping her up and taking her inside to his motel room.

On a sharp indrawn breath he drew back, staring down into the liquid depths of her eyes for a long, long moment. 'Ah, Livvy.' He made a sound, half impatience, half sigh. 'Where do we go from here?'

CHAPTER FIVE

SHE had no idea.

Liv took a jagged breath, just resisting the compulsion to place her hand on Adam's chest, to slide open his shirt front and then her own so she could feel the whisper of skin against skin… She shivered convulsively as her body remembered his.

Stepping quickly away, she rammed her arms across her midriff as if to block the path her thoughts were hell-bent on taking her. 'We should get back.'

Adam made a strangled sound, his dark eyes sweeping her from head to toe. 'And that's it? That's your response to what's just happened?'

A kaleidoscope of shattered dreams arced through her head. Just what did he expect? 'I don't have any answers, Adam.'

'No…' He sighed, pressing his fingertips against his eyes and then scrubbing them over his cheekbones. 'I don't either.' The only thing he did know was that by giving in to that crazy impulse to kiss her, he'd made things more complicated than ever.

When they arrived back at the hospital, Liv's mind was still spinning, her thoughts so tangled she wondered whether she would ever be able to unravel them.

She glanced at her watch. Heavens, she hadn't realised they'd been so long. Leaving Adam to his own devices, she hurried towards the nurses' station.

'Thank goodness you're back!' Suzy padded up quickly behind her. 'All hell's broken loose in here.'

'I was due for a break,' Liv countered, tight-lipped, refraining from any reference to the team's early tardiness, when *she'd* had to carry the brunt of the casualty department. 'What's up?'

'We're a doctor down for starters. A worker

out at the sawmill has been impaled by a timber stake. Stuart's gone out to stabilise him.'

'Are they bringing him in?'

Suzy shook her head. 'Stu's just called. They'll airlift the patient straight through to Sydney. But Stu will stay until the CareFlight chopper arrives.'

The two senior nurses looked at each other and grimaced.

'So, what else do we have, Suz?'

'The high-school bus ran off the road and hit a tree earlier this morning. Mick Hershaw was driving. Fortunately, he'd only just begun the pick-up from the outlying farms so there weren't many kids on board.'

'What casualties?' Liv swallowed the dryness in her throat. As always, she had to steel herself from turning to mush when children came in with injuries.

'Ambulance just arrived with three. Two students and Mick himself. Funny.' Suzy lifted a shoulder. 'I always thought he was a wonderfully safe driver. Luckily, he seems only shaken.'

'No sign of alcohol?'

'Mick?' Suzy snorted. 'Don't think so. He's the soul of sobriety when he drives that school bus.'

'So, who's awaiting assessment?' Liv slotted pens back into her top pocket.

'Mick and a fifteen-year-old female student. The third casualty was a first-former, Damon Tresize. Hit his chin on the metal bar of the seat in front of him. Luci is presently suturing him. He was pretty bloody and a bit panicked so she took him first.'

'OK...' Liv began running through the practicalities in her head. With Stuart unavailable, they'd need another senior doctor. 'I think Adam may be still about. Page him, would you? Meanwhile, I'll stick my head in on the girl. Do we have her name?'

'Teagen Lavelle. And better you than me. Mum's in there, raising hell. I reckon nothing less than Mick being sent to jail will convince her we're doing our job.'

Liv blew out a resigned breath. 'Nothing like being the meat in the sandwich. I'll see if I can sort her out.'

It was going to be one of those days. Liv recognised the signs the moment she went into the treatment room.

'About time.'

'Mrs Lavelle?' Liv queried the thin blonde woman who was hovering impatiently.

'Yes. My daughter's been injured.'

Liv turned towards the teenager on the treatment couch. 'And you're Teagen?'

The girl nodded, blocking a tear with the tips of her fingers and trying to sit up.

'Stay there, honey.' Liv squeezed her arm. 'Can you tell me where you're hurt?'

'I'll tell you where she's hurt,' the mother intervened. 'She's only broken her knee! That Mick Hershaw should be jailed for what he's done. Teagen was picked to do the solo in the dance number at the centenary celebrations tomorrow. She's practised for weeks and we had highlights put in her hair and everything— and now look at her!'

'It's not that bad.' Teagen's mouth trembled and tears began welling in her eyes again. 'I'll *be* all right to dance, Mum.'

'I'll tell you whether you'll be all right, Teagen.'

'No, I will!' The curtains swooshed back and Adam strode in. Judging by his tight-lipped expression, Liv guessed he'd overheard everything.

'This is Dr Westerman,' she jumped in diplomatically. 'Doctor, this is Mrs Lavelle and her daughter Teagen. Teagen was brought in as a result of the school bus accident this morning.'

Acknowledging Liv's information with a curt nod, Adam hitched himself against a corner of the treatment couch and asked, 'Where are you hurt, Teagen?'

'She's hurt her knee!' With an exasperated sigh, Mrs Lavelle sent her gaze heavenwards. 'How many more times do we have to explain?'

'Mrs Lavelle.' Adam folded his arms, his lean jaw set as he swivelled to address the woman. 'I'd be grateful if you'd let Teagen speak for herself. Otherwise I may have to ask you to leave.'

'You can't do that—Teagen is underage. I have to be here.'

After the morning he'd had, Adam felt his patience stretching to its fragile limits. 'Perhaps you'd like to sit quietly, then, while I examine your daughter?'

With a little sniff the mother took a couple of steps back and perched on the edge of the chair Liv held for her.

'Now, Teagen.' Adam turned back to his young patient and asked gently, 'Like to tell me what happened?'

The teenager blinked a bit and swallowed. 'I was thrown off the seat when the bus hit the tree. I landed really hard on my right knee. There were two other kids on the bus besides Damon and me, but they were down the back and just got bounced around a bit. It was all pretty scary but Mick was really good to us and got hold of our parents and the ambulance and kept us all calm…'

'I see.' Adam nodded slowly. He wasn't about to hurry the youngster, since he knew it was essential for her to debrief in her own time. Poor kid, he'd guess she been unable to get a word in edgeways since her mother had come on the scene. 'And did you feel the pain right away?'

'Mmm. My knee felt all wobbly.'

'She had to actually hop across to the ambulance!' Mrs Lavelle was clearly outraged. *'Hop!'*

Adam pointedly ignored her. 'Right. Liv, if you'd give me a hand, please, we'll get Teagen more comfortable.'

'Just relax, sweetie.' Liv smiled, easing off the youngster's trainers. Today Teagen was dressed in the school's sports uniform of shorts and polo shirt so access to her knee was made simple.

'OK, let's see, now.' Adam worked the knee slightly and Teagen gasped. His eyes narrowed. 'This wouldn't be an old dance injury, would it?'

'Don't think so. Sometimes it feels—not sore exactly...'

'But a bit uncomfortable?'

Teagen gnawed at her bottom lip and nodded.

'Could be a sleeper,' Adam said lightly. 'An injury waiting to happen.'

'Has she broken anything?' Mrs Lavelle's tone still had an accusing edge.

'No. I'm certain she hasn't,' Adam responded with studied calm. 'Teagen, you've obviously partly dislocated your patella. We'll give you some pain relief and pop it back in for you.'

'OK…' The youngster managed a shaky smile.

'So, how is high school going, Teagen?' Adam chatted on for a minute until the pain relief took effect.

'OK, I guess. I like sport a lot.'

'And how long have you been dancing?' Flexing Teagen's leg slightly, he began positioning his fingers, ready for the manipulation.

'Since I was little—Ouch!'

'Sorry to sneak up on you like that.' Adam worked her patella gently, ensuring it was relocated. 'We'll get a support bandage on that for you now. Any problems, come straight back in to Casualty. In the meantime, no undue stress on your knee. So, sorry, kiddo.' Adam gave a Gallic-type shrug. 'You won't be dancing at the centenary celebrations tomorrow.'

'This is outrageous!' The girl's mother flew to her feet. 'This was Teagen's big chance to be noticed. There'll be television cameras there tomorrow.' She took a step towards Adam. 'That Mick Hershaw should be brought to account.

He'd obviously been drinking and I hope you're going to blood-test him, Doctor. You mark my words, it'll be over the limit.'

'Do you have a medical degree, Mrs Lavelle?' Adam cut in, his voice lethally calm.

Her jaw dropped. 'Of course I don't.'

'Well, I do. So I'll decide what kind of treatment is appropriate for Mr Hershaw. Do I make myself clear?'

Blotchy patches of red stood out on the woman's cheeks. Suddenly her aggression collapsed like a pack of cards and she burst into tears.

'Mum, don't!' Teagen looked on in distress. 'It doesn't matter.'

'It m-matters to me…' Mrs Lavelle hiccuped a sob. 'I wanted this so much for you, Teagen…'

Or for herself, Adam thought. Another parent trying to live their own dreams through their child, he decided cynically before he walked out.

'Mrs Lavelle, sit down again, please.' Liv strove to restore calm. 'I'll get someone to bring you a cup of tea. I'm sure it's all been a shock for you. And I know how disappointed you must be for Teagen.'

'Yes…'

'Of course you are.' Liv passed the box of tissues to her.

'Thank you, Nurse. You've been very kind.' Mrs Lavelle's voice was muffled as she mopped up. 'You just never know what's round the corner, do you?'

No, you certainly don't, Liv silently agreed. 'Back in a tick.' She touched a hand to Mrs Lavelle's shoulder and stepped outside the cubicle to find Adam pacing restlessly.

He stared at her for a long moment, his jaw clenched, before he asked directly, 'Could you delegate someone to finish up in there, please? I'd like you with me when I examine the bus driver.'

Liv frowned. Was he expecting trouble? 'Do you need me as a witness?'

'After that performance in there?' His mouth twisted in the parody of a smile. 'You bet I do.'

'Mick Hershaw's in cube three. And for heaven's sake don't jump all over him.' Liv's rider was sharp and to the point.

'You think I came on too strongly with Mrs Lavelle, don't you?'

Liv's shoulders lifted in a little shrug. 'I'm not here to judge your interpersonal skills, Adam.'

His mouth pulled tight. Her frustration and disappointment with him were all but palpable. He rubbed at the back of his neck. Damn it. Judging by the way things had gone pear-shaped between them this morning, he'd have done better to have stayed in bed. 'Fill me in a bit, then, would you, please?'

'About Mick?'

'He's obviously well known in the town.'

'And well liked. He's in his early sixties, I think. Works tirelessly fundraising with the Rotary club and he's never brusque or cranky with the school kids.'

'How do you know that?'

'From Josh. Mick used to drive the primary-school bus,' she explained. 'He's only recently switched over to the high-school run.'

Adam frowned. 'So, is it possible he didn't know the route?'

'Not a chance.' Liv tore down that assumption

promptly. 'He's lived here all his life. But having said that…well, it's all a bit of a mystery how the accident could have happened,' she ended slowly.

'Perhaps the tyres…?'

'No way. Mick's very particular about maintenance. He'd never risk the kids' lives with a dodgy bus. It's just not in his nature.'

Adam lips drew in. This could all be more complicated than anyone thought. Various possibilities for the accident passed through his mind and, unfortunately for Mick, he couldn't discount any of them.

'I'll just hand the Lavelles over to Suzy.' Liv broke into his thoughts abruptly. 'Do you want to go ahead with Mick and I'll join you presently?'

'Ah—yes.' Adam managed a brief smile. 'Thanks for the background information, Liv. I appreciate it.'

'You're welcome—and I mean that.'

Adam jerked in a breath. He couldn't doubt her sincerity. His heart twisted as he watched his former wife hurry away. Obviously, she wanted to mend fences between them as much as he did.

He made a muted sound of self-disgust. *One unguarded moment.* That's all it had taken to mess things up. Now everything he'd hoped to achieve by this visit was in jeopardy.

Feeling as though a steel hand had taken hold of his guts, he forced his mind into neutral and went in search of his patient.

Pulling back the curtains on cubicle three, he strode in. 'Mick Hershaw?'

'Yes.' The bus driver jerked to attention.

Poor coot. Adam had seen how dejected he looked the moment he'd walked in. He'd been sitting slumped forward in his chair, his hands interlinked and hanging loosely between his knees.

'I'm Adam Westerman.' Adam offered his hand briefly, then turned aside to drag up another chair and sit opposite his patient. 'I'm covering for Dr McGregor at the moment,' he explained.

'I was hoping I could've seen Stu,' Mick said awkwardly. 'We're both in the Rotary, like.'

'Sorry about that. Stuart's unavailable just now.' Reaching one hand back behind him, Adam took Mick's chart from the rack, perusing it swiftly. 'I understand you had a mishap with the school bus this morning,' he said.

'Bit more than a mishap,' Mick responded gruffly. 'Couple of kiddies were injured.' His shoulders slumped. 'Mrs Lavelle wants me charged.'

Adam gave a huff of unamused laughter. 'Well, that's not for anyone but the police to decide. Have they been to talk to you yet?'

Mick shook his head. 'Still taking measurements at the accident scene, I reckon.'

'So, Mick.' Adam tossed the card aside and leaned back in his chair. 'How's your general health?'

'Pretty fair. I'm not one for taking sick days.'

'And what about this morning? Did you feel at any time you weren't in control of the bus? For instance, could you have blacked out just for a moment?'

Mick shook his head and then said gruffly, 'I might've got a bit confused for a couple of seconds, I suppose.'

'In what way?'

'Hard to explain.'

'Take your time,' Adam said gently. 'I'm not going anywhere.'

Mick's pale blue eyes regarded the senior doctor steadily. 'There was a bit of washout on the side of the road. I tried to steer away from it but my hands wouldn't co-operate—felt kind of weak. So I went for the brakes, but…I dunno…my feet couldn't seem to give me enough pressure. And then the bus just left the road and hit the tree. It all happened in a flash.'

'And there's no chance it was mechanical failure?'

'The bus had a full service just recently.' Mick paused, clearly waiting for Adam to start giving him some answers.

Instead, Adam swung up off his chair, glancing up as Liv came in quietly. He raised an eyebrow. 'Everything OK?'

She guessed he was wondering whether Mrs Lavelle had been placated. 'For the moment.' Liv wasn't going to let him off the hook just yet. She did think he'd been harsh with Teagen's mother. And arrogant.

Adam lifted a shoulder dismissively. There

were more important matters to be dealt with than whether or not he'd offended the bloody Lavelle woman.

He turned his attention back to his patient. 'Mick, I'm about to give you a general examination. I'll also be checking for any whiplash injury and any deficits in your hands and feet. Is that OK?'

'Guess so.' Mick sent a slightly trapped look at Liv.

'Don't be alarmed, Mick.' Liv deliberately tried to infuse lightness into the situation. 'Adam here is a fine doctor.'

Adam's mouth crimped at the corners in a dry grin. Cheeky monkey. 'Olivia, perhaps you'd be good enough to record my findings?'

'Certainly, sir.' Liv took up the patient chart, unclipped her pen and waited.

Adam's examination was painstaking. But he still wasn't satisfied. 'OK, Mick, you can hop down from the couch now.' His eyes narrowed as Mick lowered his feet to the floor.

'And that's it, Doc?' Mick looked relieved.

'Not quite. I want you to walk for me, please.

Just across to the far wall and back. Keep going until I ask you to stop.'

Mick's eyes clouded. 'I haven't touched a drop of alcohol—'

'Just routine,' Adam said easily. 'Do you have a GP?'

'Young Dr Metcalfe.'

He nodded. 'Will you walk now, please?' As the man walked, Adam looked thoughtful, his mouth compressing as he watched. 'That's fine.' He held up his hand for Mick to stop. 'Just one more thing now and we'll let you go. We'll need to take a blood sample from you.'

A few minutes later, it was all done and Mick was winding his shirtsleeve down again. 'When will I know something, Doc?'

'I'll have a chat with your GP first.' Adam scribbled something on the chart and then watched as Liv labelled the blood sample and placed it aside for testing. 'We may need you back for a CT scan, as soon as this afternoon.'

All three turned as Suzy popped her head in. 'The sergeant's just arrived to have a word with Mick. Shall I ask him to wait?'

'No need.' Adam's mouth tightened fractionally. 'We're done here for the moment.'

'Use Stuart's office,' Liv said. 'He won't be back for a while.' She smiled across at Mick and gave his shoulder an encouraging little pat. 'I'm sure a cup of tea for Mick and Sergeant Willis wouldn't go astray either, Suz.'

'I'll get Cait straight onto it,' Suzy complied cheerfully. 'Now, Mick, do you want a wheelchair?'

Mick seemed to regain his equilibrium in a flash. 'That'll be the day, lovey.'

'Come on, then,' Suzy grinned impishly. 'I'll escort you.'

Moving with quiet efficiency, Liv began putting the treatment room to rights. 'You suspect the onset of Parkinson's, don't you?'

Adam looked taken aback. 'Clever little thing, aren't you?'

'Not so clever.' Liv threw the used linen into a nearby receptacle. 'The condition is hardly uncommon. And I've seen a few diagnosed. Sad for Mick, though.'

'If it is Parkinson's disease.'

Liv flicked open a freshly laundered sheet and spread it over the couch. 'You're reasonably certain, though, aren't you?'

'It's looking that way.' Adam's lips twisted into a thoughtful moue. An uncontrollable tremor and rigidity were all classic symptoms of Parkinson's. 'Several things are pointing to his coordination beginning to falter.'

'And perhaps that's the reason he lost control of the bus,' Liv added flatly.

'Whatever, there's certainly a need for further investigation.'

Liv frowned uncertainly. 'So why the blood test? That won't help you make a diagnosis for Parkinson's. And blind Freddie could tell Mick hadn't been drinking.'

Dark humour flickered in Adam's eyes and pulled at the corner of his mouth. 'Ever heard of covering our butts, Sister?'

Liv sighed. 'It's all a bit of a mess, isn't it?'

'It needn't necessarily be,' Adam pointed out. 'If it is Parkinson's, we've the chance of diagnosing Mick early. That way we can get him on a drugs regime and physio before any irreversible damage can occur. It's unfortunate for the kids involved, of course, but none of them is badly injured.'

'Tell that to Teagen's mum!'

Adam gave a hollow laugh. 'I'd rather not, if you don't mind. I'll need to have a chat with Mick's GP. Do you know anything about him?'

Liv smiled. '*Young* Dr Metcalfe—Brad? He's been at the practice for about six months, took over his father's patients when he retired.'

'So he might have had only brief contact with Mick.'

'Who knows?' Liv shrugged. 'But there may be something on file from Dr Metcalfe senior's time.'

'Or not. And with no specific blood test to guide us…' Adam ploughed both hands through his hair in obvious frustration. 'We've no real knowledge of why that part of the brain begins disintegrating so we're still largely relying on medical practitioners' own clinical judgement of the patient's symptoms.'

'You mentioned a CT scan to Mick.'

'Yes, we'll do that and an EEG. That should

tell us what his brain waves are doing. But obviously he's going to need an MRI as well.'

'Bellreagh Hospital doesn't run to magnetic resonance imaging, I'm afraid. But you'll refer him anyway, won't you?'

Adam nodded. 'He'll have to see someone in Sydney. Stu may have a neurologist he prefers so I'll leave that up to him. Obviously the police will want to finalise their report so we may have to try and fast-track things from this end.'

Liv gave a shuddery little breath. 'People's lives can change in a few seconds, can't they?'

'And we see it more than most,' Adam concluded quietly.

'But you, especially.' Liv stopped, her teeth biting reflectively into the softness of her lower lip. She knew the kind of involved, delicate surgery he performed day in, day out. And the high degree of personal stress he must be under for most of his working hours. She looked at him sharply. 'How do you cope, Adam?'

He gave a huff of raw laughter. 'Quite badly sometimes, when things don't work out. But, thank God, those times are getting fewer and fewer. We're learning so much more now about how the body works.'

'But you really can't imagine being anything but a doctor, can you?' she came back softly.

'No...' He drew in a deep breath that came out as a ragged sigh. 'It was all I ever wanted to do.' He held her eyes for an age then looked away. 'Shame it cost me my marriage, though.'

Liv's heart wrenched. 'We've...never talked like this before, have we?'

'I suppose we haven't,' he said slowly, surprised by his conclusion. Not that they'd had much opportunity, he qualified silently, sadly— living miles apart as they did now...

Liv hesitated for a fraction and then threw caution to the winds. 'Perhaps all along we've been afraid to find out how the other felt.'

His mouth turned down. 'Or what to do about it, when we did.'

'We were young, Adam—so inexperienced.'

His brows flexed in a querying frown. 'We can't use that excuse now, though, can we?'

'I suppose not.' Her voice was husky, distorted by the tight little knot in her throat.

'Ah, Livvy…' He reached out his hand, gently drawing her to his side.

Liv felt butterflies begin waging war in her stomach as his fingers settled like a band of live wires around her wrist, her pulse beating like a wild thing under his fingertips.

And she knew that he could feel it too.

'Tell me I haven't been imagining it.' His voice sounded thick with emotion. 'It's not over between us—is it?'

'Adam…' A soft little breath left her mouth. She looked at him, studying his face, meeting the fathomless dark gaze. Her skin began to prickle and then contract. She swallowed heavily. 'We can't have this conversation here.'

'I know.' He let her go reluctantly, his mouth flattening in a resigned kind of smile. 'So— what time shall I call for you tonight, then?'

Without even realising what she was doing, Liv reached up and cupped his cheek, her thumb stroking along his cheekbone and the tips of her fingers sliding to outline his jaw and dipping into the hollow in his throat. 'About sevenish. But I'll be on a bit of a tight schedule. I have to drop Josh off at Mum's beforehand.'

'Why don't we do that together on the way to our dinner do?'

'Dinner-dance,' she corrected, her voice catching on a husky laugh. 'Josh would like that.'

Adam's look was indulgent. 'Seeing us dressed to the nines and going out together?'

'No…' The tip of her finger dallied with the top button on his shirt. 'I was thinking more of us going somewhere as a family.'

'Not much of a trip.' He made a sound somewhere between a snort and a laugh. 'From your house to Mary's.'

'But it's a start, isn't it?' Liv placed the flat of her hand on his chest, feeling the solid beat of his heart.

'Yes, it's a start,' he murmured throatily. And so much more than he would have ever dreamed possible. He brought himself up sharply, a twist of alarm ambushing him out of nowhere. What on earth was he thinking of? He couldn't afford to go fantasising about anything connected with his former wife.

In self-preservation, he stepped away from her, distancing himself physically. 'I—uh—should go and introduce myself to Sergeant Willis. And as soon as Stuart's back, I'll fill him in about Mick. Then I'm out of here for the rest of the day. Bit of business I have to attend to.'

Liv nodded, feeling disconcerted, her hand left hanging in space for a split second before she swept it into the side pocket of her trousers. She took a deep breath, dragging herself back from the giddy brink of what she'd felt was a new kind of understanding between them.

But, clearly, she'd got it wrong. Adam had switched off. Just like that. But why? The nerves in her stomach clenched. It was as abrupt and final as if he'd put up a *Don't Trespass* sign. She managed something like a smile. 'See you this evening, then.'

She certainly would. Adam's gaze narrowed for a moment. Was his former wife aware of the vibe she'd given off just now? And if she was, did she also realise the dangerous potency of it?

For a second his brain went foggy. Then he gave the faintest nod and moved to the door. 'See you about seven.'

CHAPTER SIX

ADAM'S heart was revving. He had no idea what to expect from this evening with Liv. Ever since that intense interlude at the hospital, his thoughts had been pulling him every which way.

He let his breath go in a fragmented stream of air and brought his car to a stop outside the house. At least Josh would be there to deflect any awkwardness between them, he thought with an odd kind of relief.

And it seemed Josh had already flagged his father's arrival. He flew out of the front gate and across the grassy verge to the car just as Adam slid open the driver's window. 'Hey, sport. What's up?'

'Mum's not ready.'

'That's OK.' Adam leant across and collected his suit jacket from the passenger seat. 'I'm a bit early anyway.' He swung out of the car. 'You all set to go to Granny's for the night?'

'Yep,' Josh said economically, more interested in checking out the sleek lines of the Mercedes. 'How fast can she go?'

'Fast enough.' Adam grinned and cuffed his son's shoulder playfully. 'Like to go for a spin?'

'Now?' The boy's eyes lit up. 'Just you and me?'

'Why not?' Adam smiled, jumping at the opportunity to spend some time alone with his son. He glanced at his watch, his mouth compressing for a second. 'We've plenty of time. Hop back and see if it's all right with Mum.' He let his hand rest briefly on Josh's head. 'Tell her we won't be long.'

The boy was back in flash, mission accomplished. 'Mum said it's cool. She's still fixing her hair. Can we go up to the lookout?' he tacked on, throwing himself into the passenger seat, while Adam held the door open. 'It's an awesome view from up there.'

'OK.' Adam managed a fleeting smile and wished his son had chosen anywhere but the lookout. The place held far too many memories.

Shrugging mentally, he went round to the driver's side and slid in, checking Josh's seat belt before starting the engine.

As they drove, Adam felt his mind drenched in flashbacks, each one colliding with the last. And one especially that lodged and wouldn't go away—of the night he and Liv had both come off duty at eleven. They'd driven up here to the highest point in the town. And he'd asked her to marry him...

'The lookout used to be a favourite place for your mum and me when we started going out.' The moment the words were out, Adam wished he could have hauled them back.

Josh raised his shoulders in a shrug but said nothing. Until... 'Why do you have to live in Sydney? Why can't you live here?'

In a reflex action, Adam shot his gaze towards his son and saw his own dark eyes reflected back at him. 'It's just not possible, Josh,' he said evenly. 'My work for starters. I need state-of-the art theatre facilities for the kind of surgery I have to perform.'

'You could get all your special stuff set up here.'

'But that still wouldn't work, mate.'

'Why not?'

'Because I have to be somewhere central, like Sydney, where my patients can come to me. I couldn't expect them to come all the way out here to Bellreagh, could I?'

'S'pose not.' Josh went quiet. 'But if a miracle happened and you *could* work here—would you?'

Hell's bells. Adam felt trapped, pushed into a corner by his son's relentless line of questioning. But it hardly came as a surprise. Josh was growing up fast and was perhaps just a little too wise for his age. And, inevitably, he had begun seeing the deficiencies of belonging to a family that was split down the middle.

Adam's laugh was wry, strained. 'I...guess it would depend on whether Mum and I could work things out. Oh, there's the sign for the lookout,' he said with some relief, changing gear and letting the car curve its way along the steep incline to the top of the hill.

When they reached the summit, Adam parked in the space reserved for visitors and switched off the engine. 'We can't stay long,' he warned, releasing the locks.

Josh merely nodded. Releasing his seat belt, he hurtled out and jogged across to the viewing station that overlooked the valley.

Adam took his time gazing around. Except for the picnic tables and some new signage, nothing much had changed. Certainly not the air. It was amazing. Clear and crisp, heady with the sweet smell of the wattles that edged up the hill and along the walking tracks.

'Check this out, Dad.' Josh half turned and beckoned to his father.

Adam lifted a hand in acknowledgment. A few easy strides brought him to his son's side. He looked out. The view was never-ending. Timeless. And it was still light enough to make out the multi-faceted greenness of the trees and grey-brown layers of rocks in the valley below.

Adam shook his head. 'It's fantastic,' he said, something wistful in his tone.

'The bush is magic, isn't it, Dad?'

Adam looped his arm across his son's shoulders. 'This part of it is, certainly.'

A sharp *ting-ting* echoed up from the valley floor. 'Bellbird.' Josh tipped his head up and grinned. 'Want to try a coo-ee?' He cupped his hands around his mouth to give the Australian bush call.

'That's pretty good.' Adam laughed. He felt like a kid again and made a reasonable effort with a call of his own. For a long time they were still then, looking out.

'The town's growing, isn't it?' Adam said at last. 'Spreading out. Is that a new estate over there?' He pointed to a ridge where once there had been pure bushland.

'Yeah. And if we're not careful, we're going to lose our wildlife corridor,' Josh said seriously.

'How's that?'

Josh warmed to his favourite subject. 'If the developers are allowed to build anywhere, then our native animals will lose their habitats—especially the koalas. And if we don't protect *them*, the only place we'll see them is in the zoo.'

Adam was astounded at his son's awareness. 'How do you know all this?'

'Stands to reason. And we talk about it at school. If too much stress is placed on koalas, they can develop chlamydia. They can't breed any more and they just die out.'

'Sounds to me like you want to be a vet.' Adam smiled.

'Don't think so,' his son contradicted. 'But I want to do something for wildlife. I'd probably have to go to uni first, wouldn't I, and get a degree in something?'

'I'd say so, yes.' Adam nodded seriously.

'But I wouldn't want to be stuck in a lab,' Josh emphasised. 'I'd want to be out in the field, doing practical stuff.'

'Well, we'll have to make sure you get the right advice when the time comes for you to begin high school, won't we?'

And maybe, just maybe, he could have some input into that decision. Adam's look was thoughtful as they drove swiftly back to town.

Liv was ready and watching out for them.

'Not late, are we?'

It had been ages since she'd seen her former husband dressed up to the nines. And now, lightened by an apologetic smile, his good looks blazed unchecked and her stomach tilted.

'I'll forgive you.' Liv's own laugh was a bit strangled. She hadn't known what to expect but there seemed no residue from Adam's odd mood at the hospital earlier. And it was good to see him interacting so naturally with their son. She felt grateful for small mercies. 'Collect your backpack, honey,' she directed Josh, a smile still in her voice. 'We have to get moving.'

'What about my band uniform?' Josh yelled as he sped down the hall to his room.

'Already at Granny's,' Liv called back.

Adam's mouth quirked. 'Band uniform?'

'He's in the school band.' Liv kept her voice low. 'They're leading the street parade tomorrow.'

'What does he play?' Adam's tone was softly amused.

'Trumpet. And not very well.' She put a finger to her lips. 'But I guess we have to give him A for effort.'

Adam nodded. 'He's a great kid, Liv. You've done a marvellous job.'

His quiet words of praise meant more to her

than she could say. 'You've had an influence, too, Adam.'

'I hope so.' He smiled and his gaze ran over her. 'You look lovely.'

'Thanks.' Liv blushed faintly. She felt good in the cornflower-blue chiffon dress. It had the fashionably new bias-cut skirt and the tiny straps over the shoulders made it cool and feminine. And so what if the neckline showed a hint of cleavage? It had been ages since she'd been anywhere or dressed up for anyone special—like a former husband. 'I bought the dress last time I was in Melbourne, visiting Jacqui.'

'You still see her?'

She nodded. 'Couple of times a year.' Their eyes met and Adam's quizzical look impelled her to add quietly, 'The city doesn't swallow me up the way it used to.'

'I'm glad about that.' He reached for her hand and squeezed it for a second.

'Our son is really into this wildlife business, isn't he?' Adam said. They'd dropped Josh at his grandmother's and were heading towards the

civic centre where the dinner-dance was being held.

'It's an absorbing hobby for him,' Liv agreed.

'Oh, I think it's much more than that.'

She blinked in surprise. 'He's talked to you
about it?'

'This afternoon at the lookout.'

'You went there!' Liv was appalled to hear a
catch in her voice.

He gave a ragged sigh. 'Liv, I didn't much
want to go either, but Josh asked especially.'

Liv felt emotion burn at the back of her throat,
stinging her eyes. 'So…what exactly did you
talk about, then?' she asked carefully.

'Josh did most of the talking. In fact he
startled me with his knowledge. I got the impression he wants to make a career in wildlife
biology.'

Liv found a light note from somewhere, not
about to let on he'd thrown her completely.
'Maybe it's just a phase he's going through.'

'Far from it.' Adam joined the line of cars that
were queuing to enter the outdoor parking lot
beside the civic centre. 'I think he's absolutely

serious, about it. So serious in fact, I think we need to begin sorting out what subjects he'll have to take to give him the right path to university.'

Liv moistened her lips. 'All right. I'll look up something on the net.'

Adam nosed the car into a parking space. 'Leave it to me, Liv. I'll have a word with Martin Burow at Kinross when I get back to Sydney.'

At the mention of the elite private school, Adam's old school, Liv felt a flutter of apprehension. 'I could just as easily have a chat with the high-school principal here.'

'I know, but let's do it my way, please? Marty's the course advisor at Kinross these days. He and I were in the same year. We still meet socially. He'll take a personal interest in our son's career aspirations.'

Liv had no comeback. And on the face of it, it seemed a sensible idea. Why, then, did she suddenly feel threatened in some way? Her instincts sharpened as a new thought struck her and suddenly she felt relief wash over her. It was probably just Adam wanting to be more *hands-on* with Josh's upbringing, as he'd told her he wanted to be…

'Ready?'

'Sorry?' Liv started, dragged back to reality by Adam's voice.

'We've a function to attend, I believe.' His hand came down and wrapped over hers.

She nodded, throwing him a distracted smile, then waited while he went round to open the passenger door for her. Was this a huge mistake? Liv gave a wary look around her as she swung out of the car.

Adam took a moment to lock the car with his remote control and then turned to her, taking her hand firmly. 'Don't look so worried.'

She met his gaze and looked away again. 'I…hate being the centre of attention—stared at.'

'Who says we will be?' he countered softly, his thumb idly caressing her pulse point. 'Come on, Livvy.' His voice was a low murmur, a gentle, coaxing sound that had her leaning into him for just a second. 'I've been about the place for a couple of days now. The shock value will have worn off. Anyway, I'm sure folk have better things to do than stare at us.'

'I suppose you're right.'

'Of course I am.' His mouth quirked in a teasing smile. 'Let's just have a good time. And look at that.' He tipped his head back, his hand moving in an all-encompassing arc above his head. 'I haven't seen stars like this for years.'

Wordlessly, Liv followed his lead and felt her heart contract. The slender moon looked almost like an intruder amongst the canopy of stars scattered far and wide like so much fairy dust in the sweep of the enormous heavens.

'Amazing.'

Liv felt his fingers tighten on hers. 'Yes…'

'Hey, guys! You spending the evening stargazing or coming inside?'

Adam and Liv spun round to see Suzy and her husband Drew moving across from their farm utility to join them. Suzy introduced the two men, adding with a chuckle, 'Adam's our hotshot city surgeon.'

'You're probably much more at home with

these kinds of dos than I am, mate,' Drew said mournfully, as they shook hands. 'I hate getting dressed up,' he lamented, easing his shirt collar as if it was choking him.

That remark earned him a jab from Suzy's elbow. 'Behave,' she joked. 'To hear you, anyone would think we lived like Ma and Pa Kettle on the farm.'

Adam laughed. 'I pretty much agree with Drew. I think ties are a useless bit of gear at the best of times.'

Suzy howled. 'Don't encourage him!'

Liv's apprehension began to fade. With a sense of unreality she allowed herself to be swept along, and under cover of the friendly banter the group made their way almost unnoticed into the function room.

Slightly overwhelmed, Liv took in the scene, smiling at the sea of faces. Fluttering a wave here and there. And it seemed as though everyone had dressed up and put their best efforts into making the evening memorable.

The seating was at large round tables. 'Oh, look, there's our gang and there's Stu waving at us,' Suzy said happily. 'Let's hope we're all sitting together.'

Much to Liv's relief, they were. And more relief followed when she found herself seated next to Helen McGregor.

'How lovely Adam could be here for the celebrations.' Helen turned her fair head towards Liv. 'And for Josh to have some time with his dad. How is the little pet?'

Liv smiled. 'Not so little, Helen. He's twelve years old now.'

'Of course!' Helen made a small face at her lapse. 'Josh is almost the same age as our youngest, Fleur.' She looked to where her husband and Adam were engaged deeply in conversation. 'It's very kind of Adam to stand in for Stu while we have this break away.'

Liv drew in a shaky breath. 'He's happy to do it, Helen.'

There was a long pause which Helen broke with gentle warmth. 'And what about you, Liv? Are you glad Adam's going to be spending this extended time in Bellreagh?'

'Well, it'll be good for Josh,' Liv deflected.

She wasn't about to tell Helen that on the question of herself and Adam, she felt enveloped in a sea of uncertainty.

'Oh, look,' Helen whispered, nudging Liv's forearm. 'Doug's getting up to speak.'

Liv watched as the mayor, Doug Wheelan rose to his feet. After a short speech of welcome in which he invited everyone to kick up their heels and enjoy the evening, the party began to get under way.

The food was set out buffet-style. It was real country fare with enough variety to please everyone, from the traditional roasts and seafood to the more adventurous dishes like the leafy pumpkin salad and sweet potato pilaf.

'Leave room for dessert,' Suzy announced to the table at large. 'They're to die for.'

'I'm a pushover for sticky date pudding,' Stuart admitted sheepishly.

'I'm partial to a bit of rhubarb fool myself,' Drew chimed in.

'Grilled mango cheeks with buttered rum has great street cred,' Adam contributed seriously.

Suzy rolled her eyes. 'Who *are* these people?'

she demanded, and then gave an irrepressible smile. 'Just don't stuff yourselves so full with dessert you can't dance, that's all.'

'You're telling me I have to dance?' Drew sent his wife a terrified look.

The company laughed as one and with the evening continuing in the same light-hearted vein, Liv found her nerves settled somewhat and cautiously she began to enjoy herself.

Later on, with most of the food sampled, couples began drifting onto the dance-floor until there were just Adam and Liv and the McGregors remaining. Suddenly, Adam tilted his head as if listening and got to his feet. 'This sounds like something we could manage, Helen, if you're game?'

'You bet. I haven't danced in ages.' Helen dimpled at her husband. 'Stuart always maintains he's got two left feet.'

Adam frowned. 'Funny, I've never noticed that. Perhaps we could do an article for the *AMJ* about the phenomenon, Stu—when you're ready.'

'Get out of here, the pair of you.' Stuart chuckled and waved a dismissive hand after them.

Watching Adam whirl Helen onto the floor, Liv felt suddenly shut out. Why hadn't he asked *her* to dance first? She turned away, managing a stiff little query. 'More coffee, Stu?'

'Thanks.' Stuart fixed his kind grey eyes on her. 'You OK, Liv?'

'Fine.' She faked a bright smile. 'Helen looks wonderful, doesn't she?'

'Not bad for having produced five children,' Stuart agreed with a wry chuckle.

Liv picked up the silver pot and refreshed their coffee. 'What's it like, having such a large family, Stu?'

'Expensive,' he quipped. 'And terrifying. But mostly wonderful.' He lifted his cup and took a thoughtful mouthful of his coffee. 'How are things going with you and Adam?'

Liv rocked her hand. 'A bit of swings and roundabouts at the moment, I guess.'

'Perhaps it's time you both took a serious look at reconnecting.'

Liv felt her heart begin to pound. In one way she supposed they had already *reconnected*. In her mind's eye, she remembered the sweet shock of his kiss that morning. But one kiss was only an infinitesimal step in the journey towards reconciliation. 'I think we're a long way from that, Stuart.'

'Why? Adam isn't involved elsewhere, is he?'

'He says not.'

'You?'

Liv swallowed through a hard little laugh. 'When would I have the time? But it's not that simple.'

'Maybe it is…' Stuart gave her a shrewd look '…if you've merely buried the love you once felt for one another and not lost it altogether.'

Was it possible? More to the point, was it what either of them really wanted? 'Adam and I have closed so many doors—'

Stuart's large hand closed over hers. 'Olivia, there was never a door that couldn't be broken down.'

Liv had a mental picture of herself and Adam armed with axes and doing just that. She shook her head at her boss. 'You're full of wise sayings, aren't you?'

He shot her a wry grin. 'Just full of it, more

like. Uh-oh!' The smile faded from his face as he glanced towards the door. 'Now, what could Sergeant Willis want?'

'I'd guess he's not here for the dancing,' Liv surmised, watching as the police officer made his way towards their table. 'He's in uniform.'

Stuart sighed. 'Is it too much to ask for just one night off in this place?'

Adam had also noted the sergeant's arrival. Trouble, he speculated by the man's purposeful stride. Drawing Helen gently aside from the other dancers, he said quietly, 'I think Stu might need a hand. Let's go back to the table, shall we?'

'Oh, no!' Helen whispered hoarsely, her hand going to her throat when she saw the policeman. 'I hope it's not one of the children…'

They arrived at the table in time to hear the sergeant say grimly, 'Sorry to trouble you, Stuart, but a four-wheel-drive's gone over the edge on the road up to the lookout. It's young Troy Saxelby and his girlfriend, Kelli Holland.'

Liv flinched. Troy taught the physical education and sports at the school and, through Josh's involvement in most of the young man's classes, she knew him quite well.

Adam said sharply, 'Injury-wise, what details do you have, Sergeant?'

'Unfortunately, nothing specific, Doc. My constable Curtis Logan, is at the scene. He was able to ascertain the driver's unconscious.'

'Ambulance there?'

'Should be by now, and the SES. But I reckon they'd prefer to have a doctor's assessment before they move anyone.'

'Right.' Stuart was already on his feet. 'I'll just get myself organised.'

'Stu, I'll go.' Adam put his hand firmly on the other man's shoulder. 'You and Helen deserve your evening out. Besides, it's the hospital's fundraiser. You should be here.'

Stuart wavered for a second. 'Well—OK, then, if you're sure?'

'I'm sure.' Adam was definite.

'Swing by the hospital on your way and pick up a trauma pack,' Stuart instructed. 'And call me immediately if you need a hand.'

Adam nodded. 'Will do.'

'We'll drop Liv home,' Helen offered quickly. Liv snatched up her clutch bag from the table. 'Thanks, Helen, but I'll go with Adam.'

CHAPTER SEVEN

'I didn't expect you to come haring off on this jaunt with me, but thanks.' Adam reversed quickly out of his parking spot and turned the car towards the town proper.

'It's no big deal,' Liv said with a tiny shrug. 'I might be able to help.' And if she was being totally honest, she'd been glad to leave the party. Watching Adam dancing with someone else, even someone as sweet as Helen, had upset her far more than she could have imagined.

'My place is on the way so could you drop me off, please? I'll change into something more suitable. You can pick me up again on your way back from the hospital.'

Adam grunted a reply, his thoughts flying ahead. Heaven only knew what they'd find when they got to the accident scene. And it had been ages since he'd had to attend an MVA. But you never forgot…

Back at the house, Liv changed quickly into jeans and a long-sleeved T-shirt. Thank goodness it was a clear night, she thought, ramming her feet into a comfortable pair of trainers. She hooked up her shoulder-bag containing her keys and wallet and ran out the front door, just as Adam pulled up.

It took them barely minutes to get to the lookout. The police had set up a road block, and the state emergency service personnel had already lit the area with floodlights that showed clearly where the vehicle had veered off the road on the lower side of the hill and rammed into a culvert.

Liv swallowed the lump in her throat. 'Adam—'

'Let's not hang about,' he said curtly. 'And stick with me, Liv. I'm going to need you.'

They swung out of the car and Adam grabbed the trauma kit from the boot.

'Hey, there, Liv!'

'Curt…' She recognised the police constable as he jogged towards them. She introduced

Adam briefly, adding, 'Dr Westerman is helping out at the hospital.'

'Right.' Curtis offered a firm handshake. 'Thanks for coming, Doc.' He began to lead the way back down to the vehicle. 'Kelli was able to tell us a roo hit them. One of those big fellas we get up here occasionally. He came right out of the blue. Troy had only a second to react. The kangaroo's gone right up over the car's bonnet and the rest, as they say, is history.'

'Are we able to get access to our patients?' Adam's query was clipped. He'd ask about the fate of the kangaroo later. Josh would hear about it and would want to know the details.

'The SES guys have managed to get the doors open and rigged up a light of sorts. Troy's in a bit of a mess.'

From an untrained eye, that could mean anything, Adam thought grimly. He took a moment to glance around him. Earlier, when he'd been here with Josh, the place had been steeped in peace and tranquillity. Now the atmosphere was almost eerie, the night shadows of the trees resembling grotesque giants in the moonlight…

Enough.

They had a job to do.

The town's two ambulances were already in attendance.

'What've we got, folks?' Adam broke open the emergency kit and yanked out a torch and stethoscope.

'Kelli seems OK,' Ben Vellacott, the senior ambulance officer, said. 'Shocked, of course. Troy's just come round. Groggy but orientated to time and place.'

'Good. I'll have a look at him first. Liv, see what you can do for Kelli, please.'

Kelli looked pale and haunted. 'His poor face…'

At once Liv could see that the relentless force of the impact had sent Troy's face slamming into the steering-wheel, smashing both cheekbones. Although the injury looked bad, she knew reversing depressed cheekbones was a relatively straightforward procedure. 'Kelli, I'm Liv. I'm a nurse at the hospital. Can you answer a few questions for me?' Liv began a simple test of the young woman's competency and checked her pulse and pupils. 'That's fine. Now, let's get you out so we can make you more comfortable. Do you hurt anywhere?'

Kelli's eyes filled. 'Just shaken, I think. I managed to brace myself.'

'Good girl. But be prepared for the possibility of whiplash in the next twenty-four hours. And maybe some bruising from your seat belt.'

Kelli grimaced. 'Do I have to go to hospital?'

'Yes. You'll need to be checked over properly and, as a precaution, we'll put you on a special stretcher.'

Liv pulled her head out of the wrecked front section of the car and addressed the ambulances officers. 'We'll need a spinal stretcher and hard collar, please, guys.'

While they waited, Liv held Kelli's hand and encouraged her to talk, asking, 'How long have you and Troy been going out?'

'Few months.' Kelli blinked away a tear. 'We'd been for a swim and we'd got fish and chips. Then Troy had the bright idea of coming up here and having a moonlight supper...'

'Oh, dear.' Liv peered closer and saw where the

young people's food had ended up in a squashed heap on the floor of the car. 'Are you starved?'

Kelli gave a weak laugh. 'Not any more.'

Ben and his partner, Carol, arrived with the stretcher.

As she was being carefully lifted, Kelli put out her hand and grasped Liv's forearm. 'Can you find out how Troy is for me, please?'

Liv covered the other's hand with her own. 'Of course I can,' she said, and waited until Kelli was safely installed in the ambulance, a space blanket ensuring she was kept warm. 'Hang on a bit, please,' she said to Carol. 'I'll get the latest on Troy before you take off.'

Skirting the cluster of emergency vehicles, Liv hurried round to the driver's side of the wrecked car. Adam was bent over his patient, the harshness of the makeshift lighting emphasising his intense concentration. 'How is he?'

'BP stable, no sign of internal bleeding. Fractured cheekbones, as you can see.'

'Leg's killing me, Doc.' Troy's mouth was contorted with pain.

'That's because you've busted your kneecap, old son.'

'That's the end of me—I'll be out of a job.'

'Rats to that.' Adam's mouth compressed. 'We can put you back together as good as new.'

The young man's teeth began chattering. 'Y-you reckon?'

'I'm a surgeon, mate. Would I lie? But right now we'll get you a bit more comfortable and on your way to hospital. Would you draw up twenty-five milligrams of pethidine, please, Olivia?'

Liv obliged and then swabbed the site and watched as Adam sent the painkiller home in one swift jab. 'Kelli's worried about Troy,' she said in a quiet aside. 'Could you have a quick word?'

'Sure.' Adam eased back out of the wreck. 'She OK?'

Liv filled him in quickly. 'Troy will need surgery, won't he?'

'Yes. I'll do it. I'll have to wire his patella and reverse the depressed cheekbones. What about anesthetic?'

'Nick Dennison should be available. His

wife's about to give birth so they're staying close to home at the moment.'

'Good.' Adam's head came up questioningly. 'Could you scrub for me?'

Liv looked uncertain. 'Shouldn't you put a call out for one of the theatre sisters?'

His dark brows snapped together. 'And risk getting someone less than sober from the dinner do? Don't think so. At least I know you and I aren't compromised.'

Liv knew that, too. She and Adam had barely touched their wine, preferring the iced water that had been in plentiful supply in large jugs on the tables. But scrub for him? 'It's a while since I was in Theatre, Adam.'

'It should be straightforward surgery. I can guide you.'

Liv's heart gave a sideways skip. She'd never have thought in her wildest dreams that the evening would end like this. That she and Adam would be caught up in a medical emergency and be working side by side in Theatre.

* * *

In the little annexe to the scrub room, Liv helped Adam gown. 'What size gloves do you need?'

He sent her an abrupt look from under his brows. She'd forgotten, and the fact that she had hurt like hell. He gathered himself. 'Eight and a half, if you can manage it. If not, I can get by with nine.'

Liv took a calming breath. 'Glove sizes I can manage.' She only hoped she could reactivate the necessary skills to provide the kind of back-up a surgeon of Adam's calibre would expect.

'Right, he'll do. Thanks, both of you.' Adam inserted the last suture in Troy's knee and signalled for Nick to reverse the anaesthetic.

Automatically, Liv handed Adam the non-stick dressings to seal the site. She'd been pushed to the limit, she acknowledged silently, but, despite a few glitches in the beginning, she and Adam had managed a reasonably coordinated effort.

He'd been patient and precise, so that after a while they'd got into a kind of rhythm and Liv had found she'd been able to anticipate what he'd need even before he'd requested it.

'Hey, you guys make an awesome team.' Above his mask, Nick Dennison's bright blue eyes lit with good humour. 'Any chance you could come on board permanently, Adam?'

'Unlikely,' Adam replied smoothly. 'And you don't have to sell me on the place, mate. I finished my internship here. It's still a great little hospital.'

'Isn't it just? Rowie and I hope to stay on and bring up our kids here.'

'Nice thought.' In an almost studied movement Adam raised his head, meeting Liv's faltering gaze. He lifted an eyebrow, telegraphing a kind of pseudo-scenario. Was she thinking the same as he was? he wondered. That if he'd been willing to return to practise in Bellreagh, their lives could have had the same kind of predictability?

Under his mask, his mouth tightened. They'd never know now. 'Right, our lad's coming round.' He slid back into professional detachment. 'Let's get him through to Recovery, shall we?'

'Not too daunting, was it?' Adam asked lightly, when he and Liv were back in the anteroom.

'No,' she answered honestly. 'You're very good to work with.'

He gave a rough laugh. 'You sound surprised. Did you imagine I'd throw things and yell at you?'

'I hadn't actually thought about it, Adam. Why would I? Your professional world is a long way from mine.'

'Well, that's put me in my place.'

'It wasn't meant that way.' Her heart skipped a beat. She didn't want to have this pointless kind of conversation with him. 'Cup of tea?'

He shook his head. 'I'd do almost anything for a decent cup of coffee, though.'

'Come home with me, then, and I'll make you one.'

'I'd like that—if you're sure?'

She nodded, her throat suddenly too dry for speech. In a millisecond time had slowed, allowing an almost tangible sense of expectation to materialise between them.

Adam couldn't take his eyes off her, a rip of desire shooting up his spine. And suddenly, urgently, he wanted to take her to him, to print a river of kisses across her throat to her jawline, to wind his fingers through her hair, using the impetus to draw her closer and closer until his mouth was on hers…

'Adam?' Liv's heartbeat sped up a notch. She swallowed thickly. His face was near—too near.

'Sorry.' He looked startled, his hand snapping up to drag off his theatre cap. 'Let's get out of this clobber and hit the showers.'

'Yes. Uh—meet you back at the nurses' station.'

They were silent on the way home. And remained silent even after Adam had pulled into the driveway and cut the engine. Was she having second thoughts about inviting him in? he wondered. His heart contracted. Probably second and third thoughts.

Finally, he could stand it no longer. Releasing his seat belt, he turned to her. 'Changed your mind, Olivia?'

'Why didn't you dance with me instead of Helen?'

'Why…?' He seemed startled by the question.

Dipping his dark head, he tightened his grip on the steering-wheel. It took an age for the words to come. 'I didn't trust myself.'

'I don't understand.'

'Hell, Livvy.' He gave a raw laugh. 'Can't you guess?'

'Oh!' Liv felt a warm tide of colour flood her cheeks. His reasons were so far from what she'd imagined. 'I thought you were shutting me out.'

'I'm sorry you thought that,' he said gruffly, his hand coming over and covering hers where it lay on her thigh.

Liv took a shaken breath, feeling the warm slide of the ball of his thumb across her fingers before his larger palm totally engulfed them.

'There's nothing stopping us from having our dance now, is there?' he asked softly. 'Away from the crowd?'

'I—I suppose not.'

'Good.' He raised her hand and kissed her knuckles. 'Got some music?'

She looked at him in the subdued light from the streetlamp, seeing the crease in his cheek as he smiled, and quickly lowered her gaze to blot out the all-male physical imprint. 'I'm sure we could find something.'

Out of the car, they made their way across the front lawn and mounted the short flight of steps that led to the patio. Liv handed him her key and waited while he unlocked the front door. He stood back for her to enter and then followed her inside.

Liv had left the two vase-style lamps burning and now their soft glow was reflecting the colours of her purple and turquoise Indian cotton cushions on the couch and bringing the simple elegance of the furnishings into soft relief.

She said thinly and too quickly, 'Make yourself at home. CDs are over there by the stereo. I'll just change out of my jeans.' She took the few steps along the hallway and pushed open the door of her bedroom, her hand going to her heart as she steadied her breathing.

Almost dazedly, she looked about her. The dress she'd changed out of so hurriedly earlier was draped across the bed and her sandals lay in a strappy heap on the floor.

She bit her lip. Would it be too over the top to put on her party gear again? Just to have a dance around the lounge room? Probably. But she decided to anyway.

Her nerve endings were violently receptive when she made her way back to the lounge room. 'Ah…' Adam let his breath go in a long exhalation. His dark eyes narrowed. Then his mouth twitched. 'I see we're dressing up for our dance. Should I put my tie and jacket back on?'

Liv's heart was swooping like a drunken butterfly. 'Are we crazy, Adam?' she blurted.

His gaze widened and darkened. 'No, Liv, we're not crazy,' he answered gravely. 'I found some music.' He held up a compact disc for her inspection.

'It's a compilation of love songs.' In a nervous little gesture, she laced her fingers in front of her.

'We can handle that.' His mouth curled slightly.

Liv swallowed the sudden dryness in her throat. 'Shall I make the coffee?'

'Coffee can wait.' He bent and pushed several buttons to activate the sound system. Then, turning, he held his arms out towards her.

Liv felt as though her shoes were stuck in wet cement. Yet her body ached for him with a shocking intensity. And she knew…once her former husband had put his arms around her, there'd be no going back…

The husky sound of a classic song began to fill the room.

Why was she hesitating? Adam felt his senses heighten almost unbearably. Surely he hadn't got it wrong? 'Let's dance…'

She took a couple of steps to bring her achingly close to him. 'Adam…' She licked her lips and brought her focus back to where it needed to be. 'I'm not sure we should be doing this.'

His jaw worked for a second. 'Yes, we should. Please, Livvy…' He said her name on a lengthy sigh, drawing her to him, his long tapered fingers curving over her shoulders, the angle of his thumbs pointing inwards, their tips teasing the soft little hollow at the base of her throat. 'For the good times…'

Nodding wordlessly, she went into his arms.

As they danced, Liv could almost feel the tension draining out of him, replaced by something else—something more vibrant and compelling.

She moved her hands from where they were linked around his neck, placing them on his chest, startled to feel the unsteady thud of his heart beneath her palms. A gravelly, fractured sigh escaped him.

'This feels so good, doesn't it, Livvy?'

She tipped her head back, meeting the dark caress of his eyes. All at once she felt the slow heat between their bodies flaring, engulfing her. And time shot backwards so that it seemed only yesterday when they had been so young, so in love.

Husband and wife...

'You do know what I'm asking—don't you?' he asked softly.

In a second his mouth had swooped down and covered hers, the raw passion of the kiss an urgent demand for her response.

A tiny sound that might have been yes shivered in her throat and her lips seemed to part of their own accord, the touch and taste of him setting her pulse on fire.

Finally, they broke apart.

'Oh, Livvy.' He seemed to swallow painfully. 'I hardly dare believe this. And you're quite, quite sure…?'

She ran her hands possessively across his shoulders and down his upper arms, the fine cotton of his white shirt doing nothing to hide his powerful musculature.

The action seemed to ignite him and he was kissing her again—but this time a sweet tenderness she'd never known in him, even during the best and loveliest times of their marriage.

And when, moments later, he scooped her up in his arms and began to carry her towards the bedroom, she couldn't help the soft laugh that rippled from her throat.

'What?'

'Is this what's called sweeping me off my feet?'

'Must be,' he growled, putting his mouth to her throat. 'Sexy, isn't it?'

He lowered her gently into a sitting position on the side of the bed. Then, uncoiling, he shucked off his shirt in one vigorous movement. The rest of his clothes were despatched just as naturally.

Liv felt her heart beating madly. His male nakedness was so familiar and yet so new that she could only remain helplessly entranced as he began to undress her as well.

First he flicked off her high-heeled sandals, then took advantage of the flimsy straps holding up her dress to simply pull them down over her shoulders and arms. Lifting her gently upright, he eased the zip open, allowing the dress to billow around her ankles. 'You're still so beautiful,' he murmured, bending to run his tongue over the exposed swell of a breast.

Liv took a shallow breath as his hands slipped behind her, releasing the catch on her strapless bra and letting it fall away. Her lacy briefs followed. 'Come now,' he whispered hoarsely, drawing her down with him on to the bed.

They were both achingly aroused, hungry for the taste and touch of each other and thinking only that after the lost lonely years apart, they were about to become lovers again. And that it seemed miracles *did* happen after all.

But suddenly Liv felt the ragged memories pushing through the hazy mist of happiness surrounding them. She stiffened in his arms.

'Baby—what is it?' His face close to hers, Adam felt her warm tears.

'Oh, Adam…' She shuddered against him. 'I can't forget.' She sobbed. 'That awful day when I left you…'

'Forget it!' He spoke in a fierce undertone. 'Forget everything and come to me, Livvy…'

Turning to him, Liv felt her senses reawakening, materialising in the softest sounds as her every breath recorded his warm male scent, once so familiar and now so tantalisingly new.

In an instant their passion was recharged and they were stirred to their utmost depths by the almost primitive beauty of this strongest of connections, as though they'd broken through the barriers of their former lonely existence to an even deeper meeting point than ever before.

At last, passion spent, they were still. But Liv knew silent tears were coursing down her cheeks. Adam knew it too. He could taste them.

'Tell me, Livvy?'

'Reaction.' She sniffed through a strangled laugh. 'I'm OK.'

'Sure?'

'Mmm.' She burrowed in against him, her face next to his on the pillow. After a long time she murmured, 'We didn't use anything. But I'm probably safe.'

Adam cradled her in his arms as if he'd never let her go. 'I'll take care of it tomorrow.'

Liv pressed her forehead again his. 'Is there going to be a tomorrow?'

'You bet.' His voice was slurred with sleep. 'And tomorrow and tomorrow…'

Morning.

'Oh, lord! Look at the time!' Liv threw back the covers and sprang out of bed. 'Adam! Get up!' She leaned down and shook him awake. 'We have to pick Josh up by eight and assemble for this tug-of-war thing by nine-thirty!'

Adam groaned. 'How did I get talked into any of this?'

'Blame Stuart's silver tongue.'

'I need coffee, Liv.'

'Put it on, then, while I have a shower.' Liv snatched up her towelling robe from the chair.

'On second thoughts…' Adam was promptly

wide awake. He sent her a wicked smile and jackknifed out of bed. 'Think I'll forego the coffee and join you in the shower instead.'

'There's no time for any funny business,' she warned. 'We've got exactly thirty minutes.'

'Then we shouldn't waste a second of it.'

Liv scooted along the hallway to the bathroom, aware he was close behind. 'I'm serious, Adam.'

'So am I, Livvy.' Adam made a grab for her and lifted her off her feet.

She shrieked. 'Put me down!'

He did. And then closed the bathroom door on her soft laughter.

Liv turned her car into her mother's driveway and kept the engine running. Her heart flipped. Josh, resplendent in his band uniform of black trousers and shirt and maroon bow-tie, was already on the front porch, waiting for her.

'What happened?' he asked, throwing himself into the passenger seat beside her.

'Nothing.' Liv reversed out and headed towards the town centre. 'Why?'

'You're late.'

'Only a bit.'

Josh flicked up an eyebrow. 'Where's Dad?'

'At the motel, I guess. And why all the questions?'

The boy shrugged. 'I thought he would've picked me up in the Merc.'

Liv's mind emptied. 'Um…Dad did emergency surgery on someone last night. I guess he slept late.' She forgave herself for the subterfuge. 'But we'll both be there outside the post office to see you march past with the band. Wouldn't miss it. And Granny, too. Is she still getting a lift with Kathleen from next door?'

'She didn't say.' Josh set his head at an enquiring angle. His mother was acting weird. 'Did you remember to bring my kit?'

'Of course,' Liv was able to reply with some relief.

At least she'd had the forethought to organise Josh's sports strip and put it in the boot of the car when she'd got home from work yesterday. 'And I'm to leave it at the school's tent at the showground, aren't I?'

'Yep. Just give it to Mr Saxelby. He's in charge.'

'Oh!' Liv gave her son a quick glance. 'You don't know, of course. He had an accident in his car last night. He was the patient Dad operated on.'

'Will he be OK?'

'Dad did a great job.' Liv glossed over Troy's injuries.

Josh shrugged. 'Dad's *always* at the hospital.' *And why can't he be around like other dads?* was the somewhat resentful message implicit in his statement.

Liv experienced a sliver of unease, feeling guilty in some way. It was almost as though by spending those precious private hours together last night, she and Adam had unwittingly left their son outside the family circle.

The thought brought a lump to her throat. 'Your father's a doctor, Josh,' she hurried to point out. 'He can't just up and leave a patient because it interferes with his personal plans. And it was an emergency. Anyway,' she added too heartily, 'he'll be there for you today, as he promised.'

CHAPTER EIGHT

'I'VE NEVER SEEN such a crowd!' Mary Malloy's face was bright with excitement. 'Here, love, tuck in beside me,' she said, making room for Liv on the front steps of the post office. 'Adam joining us?'

'Should be here any minute. Oh…' A curl of sheer happiness sent Liv's heart into orbit. 'Here he is now.' She fluttered a wave. Dressed in navy trackpants and a light grey sweat-top, he looked fit and relaxed. And wonderful.

'Morning, ladies.' He sent them a brilliant smile. 'Almost lost you in the crowd.' He stood behind Liv and placed his hands on her shoulders. 'Hi…' He bent close to her ear. And then said louder, for Mary's benefit, 'Sleep well?'

Liv coloured slightly. 'Yes, thanks. You?'

'Like a log.'

'Oh, listen!' Mary's voice rang with pride. 'Here they are now!'

All heads turned as one and soon the school band came into view, the children stepping out confidently to the stirring strains of 'Waltzing Matilda'.

'Josh should be on this side.' Liv stood on tiptoe. 'The third row, I think. There—see?'

'That's our boy,' Adam murmured with pride, focusing his camera lens and shooting off a half reel of film in a few seconds.

'He looks so—so grown up...' Liv brought her hands up, palming the sudden wetness away from her eyes and fighting against the emotional overload of the past few hours.

Adam felt his own heart squeeze tight. His whole world had fallen into place. And he realised he wouldn't have wanted to miss this moment for anything.

The next couple of hours were filled with fun and laughter. After Liv had dropped her mother at the showground, where Mary would be helping Kathleen in the refreshment tent, she'd caught up with Adam once more and they'd assembled for the tug-of-war contest.

After much heaving from both sides and a chorus of questionable encouragement delivered from the sidelines, Adam and Liv's 'amateurs' finally managed to pull Stuart's team over the line.

'Luck—sheer luck,' Stuart protested, propped forward, his hands on his thighs as he recovered his breath.

'Don't you believe it,' Adam snorted. 'Skill, mate. Sheer bloody skill. And unlike you, Doctor, I'm not puffing like a steam engine.'

'Get out of it.' Stuart's good nature was undaunted. 'Let's see what you can do with the arm wrestling later.'

'No way!' Adam raised his hands in a blocking motion. 'I'm not being co-opted for that lark, matey. Read my lips—I'm spending the rest of the day with my family.'

'Being a bit of an optimist, aren't you?' Liv put her arm through his as they walked away.

'Probably.' His dark gaze shimmered across her face. 'Where are we committed next, then?'

'Josh's sprint and high jump. We daren't miss those.'

'Wouldn't want to, would we?' Adam gently pulled her to a stop. 'You look beautiful.' His hand reached out and smoothed her cheek. 'Was it something I did?'

Her skin warmed beneath his palm. 'You look beautiful, too,' she countered cheekily. 'Perhaps it was something we did together.'

They looked at each other for a moment, then a slow smile crept over Adam's face. 'Remind me to stop off at the pharmacy later, won't you?'

Arm in arm, they strolled on, blissfully unaware of the curious glances thrown their way.

'I'm starved,' Adam said, abruptly changing direction towards the refreshment tent. 'Think Mary could rustle up a sandwich for us?'

Liv laughed. 'As long as we pay like everyone else, I think it's quite possible.'

'Do we have time before Josh's first event?'

Liv glanced at her watch. 'Just—if we eat fast.'

Exchanging greetings here and there, Adam and Liv took their places amongst the other parents and supporters who were rapidly filling every space along the sides of the running track.

'Josh's sprint is up first.' Liv consulted her programme.

'And then how long till his high jump?'

'Hmm…according to this, about an hour.' She turned her head towards him. 'Why, do you need to be somewhere else?'

'I'd really like to slip across to the hospital and check on Troy. Reassure him a bit about his recovery prospects.'

'Oh, of course,' Liv agreed, a little shocked that she'd almost forgotten about the accident last night. So much had happened in the meantime. 'We'll have a word with Josh after his race and tell him where you'll be. As long as you're back for his high jump.'

'I will be. I realise how important me being here is to our son, Livvy.'

Liv nibbled the edge of her bottom lip. 'I know. Um…I could probably lend a hand with the refreshments while you're at the hospital—unless you need me to come with you?'

'I think I'll survive.' He snaked an arm around

her shoulders, his eyes touched with laughter and firmly banked desire. 'Just.'

Adam wasn't surprised at the swift recovery of Troy Saxelby. The young man was sports-fit and physically strong.

'What do you reckon, Doc?' Troy's face was all the colours of the rainbow but his smile was in place, white and wide. 'Going to spring me out of this place?'

'Not so fast, old son.' Adam checked the pin site. 'It's looking good but we'll need you for a couple of days yet.'

Troy shrugged philosophically. 'I know I can't rush it. How did the tug-of-war go?'

'Our team won. Beat McGregor's lot into the ground.'

Troy's look was wry and a bit wistful. 'Sorry I missed it. Kids' sports going all right?'

'You've trained them very well, Troy. From what I saw, there's some real talent there. But, then, I'd say that, wouldn't I?' Adam laughed. 'My son came first in his sprint.'

Troy returned an awkward grin. 'I hadn't

realised you were Josh's dad until one of the nurses told me. Are you just here for the week-end?'

'Couple of weeks, actually.' Adam made a note on the chart. 'We'll keep you on antibiotics for the next little while and I'll have a chat to the physio about some appropriate rehab. We'll have you back at work in no time.'

'Thanks, Doc.' Troy held out his hand. 'From what I hear, you did a great job on my knee.'

'No need for thanks, Troy.' Adam returned the other's firm handshake. 'It's what I do.'

'There are plenty of helpers here now,' Liv pointed out, as she undid the strings on her mother's apron. 'Come and watch Josh do his high jump.'

'Well, as long as Kathleen can spare me.' Mary cast a quick look up and down the trestle tables that were being used as serving counters.

'Of course she can. You've done more than your share already.'

'I'll just get my bag, then.' Mary dived into a curtained-off section at the rear of the tent. 'Are we meeting up with Adam somewhere?' she asked, linking her arm through Liv's as they made their way back to the sports field.

'Mmm.' Liv glanced at her watch. 'He should be back from the hospital by now.'

'I couldn't believe he had to operate last night.' Mary clicked her disapproval. 'He's supposed to be on holiday, isn't he?'

'Adam offered, Mum. And Stuart and Helen were having such a nice time.'

'And you and Adam weren't?'

'Of course, we were,' Liv flannelled. 'But neither of us had been drinking and it just seemed the sensible option for us to take the emergency.'

'You must have got to bed very late.'

'Mmm, latish.' Liv felt herself flush. 'Oh, look!' She took her mother's warm, capable hand and urged her forward. 'Here's Adam now.'

The high jump went down to the wire. Mentally, Liv felt herself strung tight as Josh went jump for jump with his rival. 'Oh, lord!' She pressed hard on Adam's fingers. 'How much higher can they jump?'

Adam's eyes narrowed. 'I'll be surprised if Josh makes it over the next height. The other lad is very good.'

Mary sniffed. 'Matt Henry is tall for his years and his legs are longer. But he might be in for a shock. Josh is no quitter.'

'There speaks the unbiased grandmother,' Adam joked. 'But there, see—Josh has clipped the bar—'

'Oh, and it's fallen!' Liv's hand went to her heart. 'Matt's won.'

'And they're both being very sportsman-like about it,' Adam said with pride, watching his son give the other lad a playful punch on the arm and Matt returning the gesture with gusto, until they manhandled each another into a wrestling grip that ended in laughter and them both falling over on the grass.

'He's such a good boy.' Mary's eyes were misty. 'You should be so proud of him.'

Liv swallowed and answered softly. 'We are, Mum.'

'Good. Now, I've things to do,' Mary said, a bit too heartily, pulling out a tissue and dabbing at her eyes. 'And don't worry about me. I'll get a lift home with Kathleen.'

Watching her walk away, Liv smiled ruefully at Adam. 'And there speaks the not-so-subtle mother-in-law.'

'On the contrary.' He grinned. 'I've always thought of Mary as a very wise woman.' He turned his head. 'Ah, here are the lads. Well done, both of you.' Adam solemnly shook hands with them. 'It was a close-fought contest.'

Josh grinned. 'I'll waste him next time.'

'Maybe you will,' Adam said. 'But for now, how about shouting your mate a winning drink?'

'Cool!' Josh looked at the note Adam had pressed into his hand. 'Thanks, Dad.' He looked at his mother. 'Can we get a burger and some fries as well? We're starving.'

'Go on.' Liv smiled indulgently. 'And well done from me too, sweetheart.'

'Mu-um!' Josh went red.

Adam bit back a grin and glanced at his watch. 'Your mum and I are going for a coffee. Do you want to make a time and place to meet a bit later on?'

The boys exchanged conspiratorial looks. 'There's a kind of adventure park set up for the kids.' Josh made a motion with his thumb to the far side of the showground.

'They've got trampolines and an artificial climbing wall,' Matt chimed in.

'And an awesome flying-fox,' Josh added.

Adam raised an eyebrow. 'So, you want, what, hour, hour and a half?'

'Can we have a bit longer?' Josh pleaded. 'You have to wait in line to have a go at all the stuff.'

'We'll come and find you in a couple of hours, then.' Adam gave an assenting shrug. 'And no risks, guys, OK? Off you go.'

'Thanks!'

They watched the two bound off. 'Mary's right,' Adam said gruffly, stabbing a hand through his hair. 'Our son is a great kid.'

'Yes.' Liv nodded. 'And you being here has meant the world to him.'

They turned as one and began to walk away.

'Do you want that coffee, Livvy?' he asked quietly.

She glanced at him, drawn by something in his voice and met such a look of naked longing that it squeezed her heart.

She licked her lips. 'Not really.'

'Good,' he growled softly, 'because neither do I.'

He held out his hand, and she slipped hers into it. Without a word, he led her back to where he'd parked his car.

With the engine purring, Adam looked ruefully at his hands clenched on the steering-wheel and immediately relaxed his grip. Good grief! He was acting like a juvenile. He took a deep breath. 'Um…the motel is closest and practically deserted at this time of day.'

Liv nodded, interpreting his shorthand. The closer the better. A sudden heat shot through her. Within a few minutes she and Adam would be making love.

Once inside the motel unit, Adam tossed his keys onto the coffee-table. His clothes from the previous evening were thrown carelessly across the bed and he swept them up and onto a chair.

Then he turned to Liv and almost in slow motion took her in his arms. 'Hello, again,' he murmured deeply, his mouth roaming over her eyelids, the corner of her mouth and into the tiny hollow in her throat.

Their love-making was wild and wonderful and left Liv shaken beyond words. Burying her face in his shoulder, she clung to him, feeling as though every nerve end in her body had been exposed and left quivering.

'OK?' he asked softly.

She bit her lips together and shook her head mutely.

'Me, too...' His words were a breath of sound in the quiet of the afternoon.

Sheer emotional overload sent them to sleep almost immediately. Liv woke first. 'Adam!' She shot upright. 'What time is it?'

'Not again!' Groggily, he groped for his watch. 'It's all right—it's been barely thirty minutes.'

Liv let out a jagged sigh of relief and fell back on the pillows.

'You scared the daylights out of me.' Tilting her face towards him, Adam planted a playful kiss on her mouth. 'I thought we'd been sprung.'

'Oh, please!' She gave a choked laugh, arching herself against him, delighting in the growl he made in his throat as her breasts grazed his chest.

'Ah, Livvy...' Lifting his head slightly, he smudged a series of kisses over her temple, curving a path down the side of her throat and along her shoulder line. 'I wish we could stay here for the rest of the day.'

'Mmm.' She pressed her mouth to the warm hollow between his collar-bones. 'We can't, though.'

Gently, he raised her head so they were looking into each other's eyes. 'Just a bit longer,' he murmured, tasting her throat and her ear lobe.

'Yes, please...' Her words spun out on a little sigh, before he slowly and with exquisite sweetness claimed her lips.

'Shame we don't have any champagne.' Liv gave a slightly rueful smile. They were still in his motel unit. They'd showered and were sitting at the counter in the tiny kitchenette.

'Mmm.' Adam looked broodingly into his mug of instant coffee.

'It's been a lovely day so far, hasn't it? Everything's come together so well—'

'Liv, I think we should talk.'

She swallowed through a hard little laugh. 'That sounds ominous.'

Adam's moody gaze raked her face. 'Neither of us has given any thought to what's going on here, have we?'

A breath of silence.

Liv felt a sliver of unease. She took in his clamped jaw, an odd sixth sense warning her something was suddenly, dangerously out of kilter between them. She said throatily, 'I'm…not sure what you mean, Adam.'

He scrubbed a hand impatiently across his cheekbones. 'What I mean is—where is it all leading? Do we jump in and out of bed for the two weeks I'm here and then forget any of it ever happened?'

Liv's heart began beating like a tom-tom. 'You can't throw a question like that at me and expect an instant answer.'

'No.' Adam's mouth tightened momentarily before he reached out and touched her cheek, drawing his fingers over her skin. 'There's no time, and the boys will have probably had enough by now. We'd better go.' Suiting the action to the words, he stood abruptly to his feet. Walking to the door, he held it open and waited for her to go through.

When they arrived back at the showground, Adam slid the car into a parking space and cut the engine. His hand still on the key in the ignition, he turned to Liv. 'No need for you to come. I'll round up the boys.'

'And what if I don't want to be left here like a parcel?' Liv said stiffly.

Adam made a dismissive sound in his throat. 'Don't be like this, Olivia.'

The silence between them lengthened and became thicker.

'What's happening here, Adam?'

'That's what we have to talk about, surely?'

She shrugged, too close to the edge to answer, not believing how swiftly things between them had broken down.

Adam's emotions began to show as well. 'I just know we shouldn't have rushed back into bed as though it was going to solve all our problems. And I can't believe how irresponsible *I've* been, not using any protection last night.'

And again this morning, Liv could have reminded him—but didn't. 'Stop beating up on yourself, Adam. I don't think you need to worry.' She bit her lip. Already, she could feel the niggling pain that heralded the beginning of her period.

'That hardly fills me with comfort,' he snorted.

'Are you saying it's all been a huge mistake—us being together?'

'I shouldn't have come back here! That was the mistake!' His reply was harshly muted.

'You said you came for Josh's sake,' she accused him.

'I did!' The words were wrung from him. 'But then I saw you again…' His sigh came up from his boots. 'And I wanted you.'

Liv heard his voice as if from a long way off

and slowly turned to find his eyes, full of regret searching hers. She hardened her heart. 'And you had to have it your way, didn't you, Adam?'

He gave a bitter laugh. 'I've hardly had it *my way,* as you put it, where Josh is concerned.'

Liv felt as though her heart would crack wide open. 'Don't you dump that guilt trip on me. You had choices even way back then. But you refused to take the one that would have kept us together as a family.'

'That just where you're wrong, Olivia. Where you've always been wrong,' he reiterated, his eyes slashing her like lasers. 'The way things turned out, I had no choice at all.'

'Fine.' Liv felt a hard core of anger in her chest. 'Put your own interpretation on it, Adam—the way you've always done. Now, if you don't mind, I'd like to collect our son.' She swung open the passenger door and looked back at him. 'It might be better if you left now.'

'Hell!' He slammed his hand on the steering-wheel in frustration. 'I don't want to fight with you, Olivia.'

Liv felt the tight lens of tears across her eyes and there was a lump in her throat the size of a lemon. 'I don't want to fight with you either.'

'Then let's not.' He gave a ragged sigh. 'For our son's sake, at least, if nothing else. Deal?'

'Whatever.' She lifted a shoulder dismissively.

'I'll wait, then.' His voice gentled. 'Go and collect Josh and I'll take you both home.'

'I have my own car here,' Liv reminded him.

Adam's smile slipped. 'Looks like I'm redundant, then.'

'Of course you're not.' She met his eyes levelly. 'Look, Josh seems very attached to your new car so I'll tell him you'll give him a ride home and I'll follow.'

Watching his former wife walk away, Adam tried to untangle the strands of emotion inside him. It was true, what she'd said. He had wanted her but he'd also wanted to erase the dark shadows of the past. But he hadn't succeeded. All he'd accomplished had been to create yet another set to haunt him.

He became aware of the oddest kind of pain he couldn't account for. It was as though it was all centred around his heart and squeezing the life from it.

Liv hurried back past the line of parked cars. The nerves of her stomach were gathering and clenching like fine wires attached to an electrode. Her thoughts were in chaos. I felt so close to him, she agonised silently. So—so *loved*. But obviously what they'd shared hadn't meant nearly as much to Adam. He'd all but labelled it as a mistake. Bitterness, like the tip of a sword, sat sharply in her chest.

So trapped was she by her unhappy thoughts it was several moments before she took in what the voice over the loudspeaker was saying.

Stunned, she stopped and listened. And then she was running back to the car, an ice-cold feeling of dread slithering up her spine.

'Adam!' She beat frantically on the driver's side window.

It took Adam a second to react. Like Liv's, his mind had been miles away, dwelling on the emotional mess surrounding them. And trying to decide what to do about it. 'Liv?' He shot the window open. 'What is it?'

She gestured wildly. 'They're calling for a doctor to go to the adventure park. The kids—s-someone's hurt…'

Adam was out of the car in a flash. 'Did they say that?'

She shook her head, feeling sick with trepidation. 'What else could it be?'

'Any number of things,' Adam said almost roughly. 'I'll get my bag.'

They began sprinting towards the enclosure where the adventure equipment had been erected. Liv felt her heart pounding, her breath coming in hard gasps as she kept pace with Adam's more powerful stride.

'Adam, there's Curtis Logan. He's seen us—he's beckoning.'

Within seconds they were at the young policeman's side.

'What's happened?' Adam rapped, his face intense.

'One of those freak accidents, Doc. Couple of the lads were trampolining. They collided in mid-air, banged their heads together. I'm sorry.' Curt's voice softened. 'One of them is your boy.'

'O-oh...' Liv sagged and whimpered and reached for Adam. He held her to him just long enough to say bracingly, 'It'll be all right, Livvy. Come on, now. Josh needs you to be strong here.' Lifting his head, he asked, 'Have you called an ambulance, Curt?'

'On its way.'

'Right, let's see what we're dealing with, shall we?'

All kids were resilient. Adam kept the thought uppermost in his mind as they made their way through the gathering crowd to the accident scene.

Adam hunkered down beside the injured boys, unsurprised to see the other lad involved was Matt Henry. 'Sorry, Dr Westerman.' Matt's young face was white with shock. 'It was an accident.'

'We know that, buddy.' Adam was gentle. 'Can you tell us what happened?'

The boy took a shuddering breath. 'We were jumping pretty high on the trampoline—and we slammed our heads together.' He swallowed convulsively. 'Josh dropped like a stone.'

'Oh, Adam, look at him.' Liv's face crumpled

at the sight of her son's prostrate form. 'He's so…' She came to a shuddering halt.

'Take it easy, Livvy.' Adam's even tone masked his concern. Josh should have come round by now.

'I'll see what I can do for Matt, shall I?' With a huge effort, Liv fought for—and found—control.

'Please. At first glance, I'd say he's dislocated a shoulder. Curt, could you clear a bit of space around us? And then give Liv a hand.'

Biting her lips together, Liv turned her attention to her son's friend. He looked glassily pale. 'I feel sick…' As Liv held him, Matt turned his head and began to retch miserably.

'Could we get some ice here, please?' Liv snapped the question to one of the bystanders. She suspected Matt had a fractured cheekbone and his face was beginning to swell. Smoothing the boy's fair hair back from his forehead, she asked, 'Are your parents here, Matt?'

He shook his head. 'Gone home. Josh said you'd give me a ride home later.'

'Right.' Liv did her best to stay professional, although every nerve in her body was screaming for her to be with her son. But Adam was with him and that had to be enough for the moment.

'What can I do, Liv?' Curtis hunkered down beside her.

'Could you get word to Matt Henry's parents, please? Tell them to meet us at the hospital. And don't alarm them. His injuries don't appear life-threatening.'

'Will do.' The policeman shot upright. 'I'll radio the station. They can handle it from there.'

Adam looked grim as he monitored his son's vital signs, noting Josh's pulse was elevated but still strong. Please heaven, it would be nothing worse than concussion. His mouth tightened. He'd found a darkening bruise on the small of his son's back as well. Obviously he'd hit the metal edge of the trampoline with force. It was worrying.

'Ambulance is here, Doc.' Curt waved the emergency vehicle through with all the aplomb of an officer on point duty in the busiest city.

'Right, let's get these youngsters on their way.' Relief showed on Adam's face. He'd already used his mobile to alert Casualty, gratified to know Stuart was waiting for them. 'We'll need a spinal stretcher for this one, please,' he said to the ambulance officer.

'Right you are, Doc. Got one about his size, I reckon.'

'Dad…'

'Hey, there, sport.' Adam's voice was husky with relief. 'You're awake. Mum's here, too.'

Josh blinked a bit. 'What happened?'

Adam stroked his son's cheek with the backs of his fingers. 'You and Matt were trampolining. You banged your heads together. Remember now?'

'Think so…'

'Good lad.'

'Are you taking me home?' Josh asked.

'Not right now.' Adam's mouth compressed. 'First we'll get you over to the hospital so Dr McGregor can have a look at you.'

'I'm coming with you in the ambulance, sweetheart.' Liv held tightly to her son's hand.

'What's wrong with m-me?' Josh's voice went up a note and cracked.

'You'll be fine, mate.' Adam tried to sound reassuring but it was an effort. 'We'll get some X-rays and sort you out in no time.'

'No, I mean…' The boy's eyes flew wide in fear. 'Why can't I feel my legs?'

Adam shot a look at Liv and her heart failed. In a second she knew something was wrong. Very, very wrong.

CHAPTER NINE

'THANKS for coming, Mum.'

Liv held tightly to her mother's hand. They were at the hospital and waiting for news on Josh.

'He'll be all right, love.' Mary gave her daughter's fingers a comforting squeeze.

'We don't know that,' Liv responded, a little catch in her voice. 'Adam's been gone ages.'

Against Stuart's advice, Adam had insisted on accompanying their son to the X-ray department. 'Leave it to me, laddie,' Stuart had said kindly. 'You're emotionally involved.'

'Don't lock me out of this, Stu.' Adam had been grim-lipped and determined.

Stuart had merely shrugged helplessly and hurried after the trolley carrying Josh towards the X-ray department.

'What kinds of tests will they do?' Mary asked now.

'Probably a full X-ray and a CT scan of Josh's head.' Liv felt her stomach turn over and she swallowed jerkily. 'He could end up paraplegic…'

'Oh, lovey, don't think that way.' Mary used her most rallying voice. 'Josh is a healthy boy.'

'We have to face the possibility, though.' Liv blinked back the tears that kept coming.

Mary tsked. 'Face it if and when you need to—that's my motto.' She pulled a wad of tissues from her handbag. 'Here. Blow your nose and wipe your eyes, Olivia. Josh won't want to see his mum looking like a wet weekend, now, will he?'

'No.' Liv hiccuped a raw laugh and took a shuddering breath.

'Let's get a cup of tea, shall we?' Mary got to her feet. 'At least it will give us something to do with our hands instead of wringing them and worrying about things that might never happen.'

'Terrible way to make tea,' she said a few minutes later, dangling her teabag in a paper cup of hot water.

'I could go along to the nurses' station and make us a pot,' Liv offered.

'Heavens, no. Don't be silly.' In a businesslike manner, Mary dispensed with their teabags and then guided her subdued and somewhat lost-looking daughter across to one of the tables dotted about the visitors' lounge. 'You and Adam *will* cope, Liv,' she reinforced quietly a few minutes later. 'Whatever happens.'

But not together, as parents should. Liv looked down into the murky liquid in her cup. 'How, Mum? With Adam in Sydney and me here…'

'Have you managed to talk at all?'

Liv felt the bile rise in her throat. If they'd only stopped at *talking,* perhaps things between them wouldn't be so muddled now. 'We've talked a bit and I thought we were making some headway.' She paused and gnawed at her bottom lip. 'I don't think there's much chance of a reconciliation.'

'But some, perhaps?' Mary pursued doggedly. 'Even a glimmer? Adam seemed in such good form this morning.'

That was this morning, Liv thought sadly.

Now, only a few hours on, everything had changed, broken down. 'He's still bitter, Mum. And we're still blaming each other.'

Mary sipped her tea in silence. The young people of today had no idea. She stifled a sigh. Had they never heard of the word 'forgiveness'? For heaven's sake! Adam and Liv should be rearing their son together, not living so far apart, as they did. Perhaps it was time she sat Adam down and talked to him. Like a mother.

'Oh, here's Adam now!' The flimsy table rocked as Liv scrambled to her feet. But he still looked so serious... Her heart dived. 'How is he?' she burst out, her voice reedy with apprehension.

Adam came straight towards her and took her in his arms. 'It's all right, Livvy.' He coaxed her with his hand, chafing her shoulders. 'Our boy's all right.'

'Oh, thank God!' she whimpered, and let herself surrender to the inner warmth of his tenderness.

And Adam responded, hugging her tightly to him, his face buried in her hair.

Watching Liv and her former husband, the intensity of their embrace, Mary felt a painful tightening in her own throat. Diving into her bag for more tissues, she blew her nose and got shakily to her feet. How on earth could these young people believe there was nothing left of their marriage? It was beyond her. Perhaps she'd better start praying for another miracle. The thought brought a watery smile to her face as she hitched up her shoulder-bag.

'Mary.' Adam looked up, seeming to come back from somewhere. 'Don't go.' Reaching out, he drew her into the circle.

'So, what's the prognosis?' Liv asked gently a few minutes later when they'd all calmed down. 'And when can we see Josh?'

'It's all good news.' Adam was still holding Liv's hand. He increased the pressure on her fingers. 'And we can see our boy shortly. Just now, Stu wants us in his office to explain things. You as well, Mary,' he insisted, when the older woman would have slipped unobtrusively away.

'Come in, come in.' Stuart moved quickly to usher the little party into his office. 'I've laid on a few refreshments. I think we could all do with something after the kind of afternoon we've had. Ah, Liv.' He gave her one of his special smiles. 'Mind pouring the coffee? I'm sure you'll do a much better job than I.'

Under Stuart's gentle manner, Liv found herself beginning to relax. She smiled wryly as the two men began to make short work of the freshly made sandwiches. Turning to her mother, she mouthed softly, 'OK?'

Mary nodded. 'Coffee's lovely.'

'Well, now,' Stuart said a bit later, draining his coffee and placing his cup back on its saucer. 'Let's talk about young Josh, shall we?'

'What actually happened, Stu?' Liv leant forward, her hands clasped on her lap.

The senior doctor's mouth pleated into a thoughtful moue. 'It's my opinion, and Adam agrees, that the jolt to Josh's back when he hit the metal edge of the trampoline was the cause of the temporary paralysis. I won't get too clinical, Adam can fill you in on that score, but the upshot is your boy suffered some nerve compression. It's just taking time to come good again.'

'How long?' Liv's eyes widened in query.

Stu smiled. 'Not to worry, Liv. Josh is already getting feeling back.'

'And there'll be no residual damage?'

'I'd say not. But Adam will keep an eye on things.'

'Will you keep Josh in, Doctor?' Mary wiped a swift hand across her eyes.

'At least overnight. Perhaps an extra day to make sure. He's being settled into the kids' ward now.' Stuart smiled, his eyes crinkling at the corners. 'Like to go up?'

'Do you have an update on Matt?' Liv asked Adam as they began to file out of Stuart's office.

'He's going to be fine. Pretty sore, understandably, and a bit sorry for himself. I've spoken to his parents. They want to pop in on Josh before they take Matt home.'

'That's probably a good idea for both the boys,' Mary said wisely. 'Reassure them.' She put her hand on Liv's arm. 'Love, I'm going home now. You and Adam should be with your son. And give him a kiss from his granny and tell him I'll see him tomorrow.'

'Mum, are you sure?'

Mary nodded, looking suddenly older than her fifty-six years. 'It's been quite a day. I'll be glad to get home.'

'I'll give you a lift.' Adam was already tapping his pockets for his car keys.

Mary flapped a hand. 'I wouldn't dream of it. You're needed here, Adam—*with your family,*' she emphasised clearly. 'I can ring for a taxi from the foyer.'

'At least let me pay for that.'

'That's way too much.' Mary waved away the note he'd flipped from his wallet.

'Mary, don't argue with me, please,' Adam responded quietly, pressing the note into her hand. 'You've always been here for Liv and me. Frankly, I don't know what this family would do without you.'

'Oh, tosh,' Mary dismissed. 'It's what families do—or they're supposed to.'

Liv suppressed a dry smile and leant forward to peck her mother's cheek. 'I'll call you later.'

'I can't believe he threw us out!' Liv didn't know whether to laugh or cry as they left the children's ward and made their way along the corridor to the lift.

'We'd been there for over an hour, Liv. Josh was starting to feel embarrassed with all the attention.' Adam swung his arm up around her shoulders and hugged her. 'And maybe you overdid the hand-holding just marginally,' he teased gently.

She ignored him huffily.

'Hey, don't get your mummy feathers ruffled,' he admonished with a soft laugh. 'It's a male thing.'

'He's never been in hospital.'

'He'll be fine. And the staff will spoil him rotten.'

The lift was already waiting on their floor and they got in.

'Home now?' Adam's hand came up and smoothed her hair.

'Back to the showground, more likely. My car's still there, remember?' Hardly aware of what she was doing, Liv let her head rest against him. 'I don't know what I would have done today if you hadn't been here.'

'You'd have coped. But I *was* here, and that's all that matters.' He breathed in, absorbing her scent, utterly aware of her and the reaction of his own body.

But where did they go from this point? he wondered soberly. It was obvious their bodies still called to one another—more like *screamed* to one another, he substituted grimly. Plus they had a beautiful son together. So why on earth couldn't they make the rest of the pieces fit?

The lift had come to a stop on the ground floor but Adam made no effort to release the door. A solemn light came into his eyes and he brushed the pad of this thumb against her cheek. 'May I come home with you tonight, Livvy?'

Dazed, she watched the small lifting of his throat as he swallowed, feeling a surge of oneness with him, a burst of happiness she couldn't hide. She managed a tentative smile. 'I think that could be arranged.'

'Thank you.' Carefully, he scooped a wayward tendril of hair away from her cheek. 'Then let's swing by the motel on the way to the show-ground so I can collect a change of clothes.'

* * *

When they arrived home there was a misty shower falling, leaving the faintest chill in the air. In an end-of-the-day gesture, Liv raised her arms and stretched, dragging her fingers through her hair and shaking it out.

Observing her action, Adam said evenly, 'You take the shower first and I'll tidy up our mess from this morning.'

'Thanks.' She gave him an uncertain smile, still feeling slightly overwhelmed by the events of the day. And they still hadn't *talked.*

'Glass of wine?' Adam asked when she trailed into the kitchen a bit later, clad in comfortable lightweight track pants and a soft blue T-shirt.

'Mmm, lovely.' Liv took one of the high stools at the kitchen bench. 'Thanks for doing all this.' She waved a hand around the kitchen.

'Nothing to it,' he dismissed, pouring her wine and then placing the bottle back in the fridge.

'You're not having one?'

'No. I brought some Scotch. I'll have a small one, I think.' Suiting the action to the word, he got ice cubes from the freezer, slipped them into a tumbler and sloshed the whisky over. 'Josh's accident has rather brought us down to earth with a thump, hasn't it?' He stood on the other side of the counter, looking down into his drink.

Yes. Liv turn her wineglass full circle on its stem. Arguing as they'd done earlier this afternoon now seemed shallow and a bit pathetic. She watched as a spilt drop of her wine broke into shining globules on the countertop. 'You mean, because for the first time in a long time we functioned as a family?' she said eventually.

'Something like that. And I dare to think it meant a lot to our son as well to have us both there with him.' He rattled the ice in his glass. 'From here on in I think we have to take a much more considered approach to things. Don't you agree?'

She knew what he meant. No more jumping into bed regardless of the consequences. 'You're saying we should be more circumspect around Josh?'

His jaw worked for a second. 'We can't let him think we're back together when we're not. That would be too cruel.'

'I agree entirely.'

'Good.' His mouth twitched. 'We're making headway.'

They moved quietly and gently through the rest of the evening. Liv lit some candles and put on a CD of classical guitar music while Adam took his turn in the shower.

'Did you call Mary?' he asked, coming back into the kitchen. He was still towelling his hair dry.

'Mmm.' Liv tasted something from the pan on the stove. 'I said we'd give her an update in the morning, after we talk to Stu.' She shot a quick look over her shoulder. 'I'm heating some soup. OK?'

'Sounds good.' He threw the towel aside and went to peer over her shoulder. 'What can I do to help?'

Liv's mouth tucked in on a grin. 'Think you could manage to get a couple of bowls down from the top cupboard?'

'Sure.' He found the bowls and with a little

flourish placed them on the table. Liv dished up the soup, adding a sprinkle of fresh herbs across the top. The final addition to the meal was one of Mary's homemade loaves, which they broke up. Then they ate off trays in front of the fire.

The rain continued to fall and the night drew in around them. 'Cup of tea?' Liv suggested later, swinging her feet to the floor. Somehow she'd become wedged against Adam and one of her legs had pins and needles. 'Ouch!'

'Here, let me rub it.' He hoisted her feet onto his lap and began working his fingers up and down her calf muscle. 'Better?' He gave her a fleeting smile.

'I think I'll live.'

'Stay put, then. I'll make the tea.'

'No, I should walk around,' she insisted. 'Give me a hand up.'

He did, turning her to face him, spreading his hands over her hips and looking deeply into her eyes. 'It's meant the world, being here with you like this, Livvy,' he said, his voice gruff and not quite even.

She sighed shakily. 'What you said earlier,

about slowing things between us. Did you mean you won't stay tonight?'

He searched her face and finally admitted quietly, 'I want to, but—'

'Stay.'

He hesitated.

'It'll be our last night for a while. Josh will probably be home tomorrow. Please?'

They didn't make love, simply lay together, his arms round her, her head pillowed on his chest while she listened to the steady beat of his heart beneath her ear and wished she had the power to change them into a real family again.

Close, united, happy.

When she woke, Liv was startled to see it was already eight o'clock. She blinked fuzzily. There was no sign of Adam. Surely he hadn't left without a word to her? 'Oh, lord,' she muttered, rolling out of bed and slipping into the bathroom.

A few minutes later, she found her former husband in the kitchen. He was parked at the table, his fingers laced around the mug of tea in front of him. He looked up and half-smiled. 'Hi. Tea's just made.'

'You should have woken me,' Liv scolded lightly.

He lifted a shoulder. 'You were obviously exhausted. Anyway, apart from Josh, there's nothing we have to do this morning, is there?'

'I suppose not.' Liv poured her tea, pulled out a chair and sat opposite him.

A beat of silence and then Liv said quietly, 'I've got my period so you don't have to worry.'

'Oh.'

'And that's it? I expected you to be doing handsprings. You're off the hook.'

His dark brows shot together. 'I'm relieved, yes. You have to admit it would have complicated things, Liv.'

She shrugged, feeling strangely empty. On the other hand, it might have catapulted them towards a decision about their future—whether they were going to spend the rest of their lives together or apart.

'I called the hospital earlier,' Adam said. 'Josh had a good night. They expected Stu in about now to check on him. I imagine we'll be hearing from him shortly to tell us whether we can bring our boy home.'

'We'd better get a move on, then.' Liv stood to her feet. 'Would you like some breakfast?'

'I'll make us something.' His dark gaze narrowed over her face without make-up, her fair skin, the scattering of tiny freckles, the soft, sweet fullness of her mouth. 'You get dressed, hmm?'

Liv hesitated, her hand going to the neckline of her cotton robe. 'I...um...I mean, it's just occurred to me. I wondered if you felt like moving home for the time you'll be in Bellreagh,' she said in a rush. 'There's a spare bedroom and you'd see much more of Josh. It was just a thought,' she said when Adam just sat there, his mouth clamped into a thin line.

He spoke finally, 'Are you sure about this, Liv?'

'No, not really.' She gave a raw laugh. 'But we have to do something, Adam. We can't go on in limbo. Perhaps if we try living as a family for a while, things might become clearer.'

He let his breath out on a harsh sigh. 'But

having separate bedrooms is not really living as a functioning family, is it?'

Liv's mouth dried. 'Anything else would be impossible. We've already agreed we have to be sensitive to Josh's feelings—not to give him false hope that we're back together.'

Almost impatiently, Adam heaved himself to his feet, pacing across to the window. Looking out, he seemed preoccupied, dragging both hands through his hair, pausing as he reached the back of his neck.

'All right,' he said at last, feeling the weight of the decision knocking in his chest. 'Let's give it a shot.' His mobile rang and he swung to face her. Liv's gaze faltered. The call would most likely be from Stuart to tell them he was ready to discharge their son.

But it was lot more complicated than simply going to the hospital and collecting him.

They'd have to tell Josh his father was moving home.

And once they'd set the plans in motion, there'd be no going back.

And somehow they both knew this was their

last chance to make their relationship work, to reclaim the family they'd once been.

Or let it go for ever.

CHAPTER TEN

'WELL, that's about it.' It was the following Tuesday and Stuart was handing over to Adam. 'You've met all the medical staff except our other resident, Tim Crossingham. He's been on days off. Back tomorrow.'

'What's the rundown on him?'

'He's good.' Stuart touched a few keys on his computer. 'Unfortunately, we have him for only another couple of months. Then he's off back to Melbourne.'

'He seems pretty well rounded.' Adam speed-read the information on the screen. 'That's good to know.' He spun off the corner of the desk. 'You and Helen ready to take off?'

'We're on the flight this afternoon. Over nighting in Sydney. I want to spoil Helen a bit,' Stuart added sheepishly. 'Then we fly to

Canberra first thing in the morning. Conference begins tomorrow afternoon.'

'Good. I'll keep things ticking over here, so make sure you just relax and enjoy yourselves.'

'We'll do that. I really appreciate you standing in for me, Adam.'

'Stu, stop with the thanks. We're doing each other a favour here, aren't we?'

'Well, I hope so, laddie.' Stuart began stuffing papers into a leather briefcase. He'd heard the tiniest whisper that Adam had moved back into the family home. Perhaps it was for convenience, perhaps it was something more. But, despite how much he was tempted, he wasn't about to ask.

Some things you just left alone to sort themselves out. And in this case he hoped they would sort out positively for Adam and Liv Westerman. 'How's young Josh?' he asked instead.

'Great. Back to school tomorrow. Matt, too.'

Stuart grinned. 'Young monkeys. They'll get plenty of mileage out of this amongst their mates, no doubt.' He cast a quick look around his office and, seemingly finding nothing he'd forgotten, said, 'Feel free to reorganise things in here or in the department, if you need to.'

'Stu, relax, OK?' Adam's handshake stretched into extra reassurance as he added a friendly thump across the shoulders. 'I won't let the place go to rack and ruin while you're away.'

'And I won't wish you a quiet time in A and E,' Stuart countered. 'Otherwise every man and his dog will start having accidents all over the place.'

'Even if they do, we'll cope.' Adam began to usher the older man out of his office. 'And no sneaky phone calls to check on us. You're out of here.'

Two days later, Adam was installed. As far as running the department went, he'd left things basically the same. It worked well and there was no point in making changes for the sake of it. Not when he was covering for such a brief amount of time.

From the open window of Stuart's office, he looked across the landscape to the paddocks, newly ploughed for spring planting. The turned-over soil was set out in neat patches, rather like a draughtboard, he decided with a touch of wryness, and compared the view with the one from his own office at St Christopher's in Sydney.

There, from its sixth-floor height, he looked out at high-density city surroundings. But with the benefit of air-conditioning, he was insulated from the outside world. Now, as the drone of a tractor came to him on the still air, he wondered again how his life would have worked out if he'd opted to make his life here in Bellreagh.

He exhaled a long breath that turned into a sigh. He hoped he and Liv hadn't given Josh any false hopes that they were back together as a family.

Over breakfast on the morning after his son's discharge from hospital, Adam had explained as simply as he could that while he was covering for Stuart at the hospital, he'd be living at home.

'So, will we get to do stuff together?' Josh had wanted to know. 'Just you and me?'

'If I'm not needed at the hospital, then you bet we will. Got something in mind?'

'Yep.' Josh had made milky inlets in his plate

of porridge. 'There's a father-son day coming up with the Scouts.'

'I won't have to make a fire by rubbing two sticks together, will I?'

Josh rolled his eyes. 'Get real, Dad. Reid's invited the troop to his farm.'

'Reid's your troop leader?'

'Reid Charlton,' Josh confirmed. 'He used to be a champion rodeo rider. Now he trains horses—wild ones,' he added with something like awe. 'It'll be next Saturday. I'll be OK to go, won't I?'

Adam ruffled his son's hair. 'I imagine so.'

Later, Adam had asked Liv to fill him in about the man.

'Reid's a bit of a legend around Bellreagh,' she'd told Adam. 'He rescues brumbies and trains them for the disabled. He's also a whisperer.'

'A horse whisperer? Like in the movie?'

'Apparently. And for his daytime job he makes saddles.'

'So, come Saturday, I guess I'm going to have to measure up against a real hero.'

Liv was laughing. 'Don't look so worried. You're still pretty much Josh's hero—haven't you noticed...?'

'So, Josh, what exactly is the programme for today?' Adam asked. It was Saturday and they'd left for the thirty-minute drive to Reid Charlton's property, Doonside, just after ten.

Josh's face lit up. 'Reid said he'd have a talk to us about the horses and stuff first, then we're having a barbecue and after that we'll be able to watch Reid start to tame one of the brumbies.'

'And our contribution to lunch is in the Esky, I take it?' Adam half-smiled, thinking of the cool-box he'd hauled into the boot earlier.

'We're all supposed to bring something. Mum and I made an awesome salad this morning while you were at the hospital and I put in those soft drinks you bought.' Josh sent his father a cheeky grin. 'And Reid's supplying the steaks.'

'Nice teamwork, then.'

'Yep.' Josh settled his cap back to front on his head.

Seeing the action out of the corner of his eye, Adam growled, 'That's not going to keep the sun off your face, mate.'

The boy lifted a shoulder defensively. 'All the guys do it—it's cool.'

Adam's mouth compressed. Not so cool when you're forty and having lesions treated. But Josh wasn't about to listen to a lecture about the damage caused by over-exposing his young skin to the sun's ultraviolet rays. Instead, he suggested diplomatically, 'Why don't we get you a decent bush hat?'

'Reid wears an Akubra.' Josh's look was hopeful. 'But they cost.'

'Anything worthwhile usually does. Matt and his dad coming today?' Adam changed conversational lanes deftly.

'Yep. There'll be about ten of us, I think. A couple of the guys don't have dads living with them so they come with someone else's.'

Adam felt his heart twist painfully. 'Is that what you normally do?'

'Sometimes.' Josh moved closer to the window, peering out.

'And other times?' Adam was like a terrier with a bone.

'I can always do stuff with Matt and his dad. They don't mind.'

But I do. Adam's head jerked up as if his son had activated a string. He was Josh's father, Adam thought vexedly. And he was missing out on so much of his son's life. He couldn't let it go on like this. He just couldn't.

'Look, Dad! That's Reid's place over there.' Josh pointed off-road to where a single-storey mellow-brick home nestled quietly in the mid-morning sun. 'And there's the round yards for the horses,' he said excitedly. 'I can't see any other cars. We must be the first here.'

Adam cut back his speed and eased the car over the metal grid and onto the property. He was really looking forward to the day ahead and spending time with his son.

Reid came out to meet them. He was in his mid-forties with the lean, whippy build of a stockman. 'G'day, Doc.' He held out his hand. 'Young Josh has told me all about you. How you do that special surgery on the kids.'

'Pleased to meet you, Reid.' Adam returned the handshake firmly. 'My son's told me quite a bit about you as well. You're something of a legend about the place.'

Reid coloured faintly under his tan. 'Dunno about that. I got an affinity with horses. That's about the size of it.'

'Where's the horse you're taming today, Reid?' Josh rocked impatiently from one foot to the other.

'Over at the yards.' Reid made a thumbing motion behind him. 'I've had her in there for a few days so she gets used to seeing people moving about. Then, with a bit of luck, she won't spook when I approach her.'

Adam stroked his chin. 'I can see horse whispering is quite a science. You must have extreme patience.'

'I guess. Come and have a look at her before the others get here,' Reid invited.

'Have you had her long?' Adam asked.

'About a week. She'd been running with a mob of brumbies mustered from up in the hilly country. I bought her at an auction. I thought she had potential.'

'She's a great-looking horse,' Adam agreed when they stood at the yard rails looking in at the Palomino mare with her creamy-coloured coat and distinctive white tail and mane.

'Does she have a name yet?' Josh sent an enquiring look up at his scout leader.

Reid's grin was laconic. 'I've called her Angel. Hope she lives up to the name when I start to tame her.'

A couple of hours later, they were about to find out.

Kerry, Reid's wife, joined in with the group to explain what was going on. 'I'd ask you all to remain very quiet,' she said, leading them to a viewing platform a short distance from the rails. 'We can't risk the horse taking fright and going berserk. That would be very dangerous for Reid. I'll give a brief commentary as we go along while Reid puts Angel through her paces, but feel free to ask me to explain anything about the procedure.'

After a bit of mild shuffling, the group became still, all eyes turned towards the yard as Reid opened the tall gate and entered quietly.

'Why is he carrying a whip?' one of the boys asked with a frown. 'He's not going to hit Angel, is he?'

'Not at all.' Kerry's modulated voice carried clearly to the group. 'Reid will merely flick the whip to encourage the mare to run around the yard and to teach her to face him and to feel safe.'

The group watched spellbound as Reid repeated the procedure over and over until the mare was ready to come close.

As he stood perfectly still, Angel tentatively stretched out her muzzle towards Reid's hand and nudged him in a moment of human-animal trust.

Beside his father, Josh murmured with something like awe, 'It's magic…'

In silent communication, Adam leaned over and put his hand on his son's knee and squeezed.

'Lesson number two coming up,' Kerry said quietly and they watched as Reid lobbed a training rope over Angel's neck.

Initially, the young horse reared violently, fighting the tether, but after a few minutes she was trotting around calmly and trainer and horse were facing each other again.

'That's all Reid will put her through today,' Kerry said. 'Angel will continue training for another four weeks, have a month off, then have four more weeks' training.'

'What will happen to her then?' Josh's voice carried a hint of concern.

Kerry smiled. 'Reid is hoping to prepare her to become a child's pony.'

'Had a good day, sport?' Adam asked as they drove home.

'Yep. Did you?'

'Mmm. Pretty impressive stuff, wasn't it?'

Josh blocked a yawn. 'Animals are great. I hope I get to work with them some day. Did you like animals when you were a boy?'

'I wasn't around them much.' Adam's gut wrenched. Pretty soon conversations like this with his son would be via the telephone again. Or non-existent. His time in Bellreagh was rapidly coming to an end. And then what? So many decisions still had to be made and finding the right answers was like trying to capture an elusive sunbeam.

His hands tightened on the steering-wheel. There was one decision he was certain could be made fairly quickly though. The matter of Josh's high-school education.

'Nasty wound.' Adam turned from washing his hands at the basin. It was Tuesday, and they'd just treated a worker from the cannery who had presented with a hand injury from a broken piece of metal on the edge of a conveyor system.

'Poor man.' Liv quietly went about putting the treatment room back to rights. 'Being a diabetic won't help his recovery rate either.'

'We might have to get the maggots in.'

Liv shuddered. 'Oh, please!'

'Works, though. Uh, I wondered if we could go out for a meal this evening.' Adam changed the conversation abruptly.

'You, me and Josh?'

'No. Just you and me.'

The implacability in her former husband's voice spun Liv's gaze back towards him and the atmosphere between them was suddenly as taut as a tripwire. Her heart thumped. 'You make it sound urgent.'

'It is. Time's running out and we've decisions to make about the future of this family, not the least of them being where our son is going for his high-school education.'

Liv's thoughts began spinning, fracturing like ice under heat. She'd been dreading this moment but the look on Adam's face told her there was no hope of it being postponed. 'I'll ask Mum to feed Josh, then.'

'I've already done that.' Adam's rejoinder was bland. 'If you don't mind a pub meal, the Royal is under new management. Tim says the grub has improved a hundred per cent.'

'All right.' Liv felt her heart squeeze tight and she wondered why they were bothering with a meal at all. With the kind of conversation they were likely to have, she doubted she would be able to swallow anything resembling food.

'We could just as easily have had this discussion at home,' Liv said stiffly. It was a little after seven that evening. They'd dropped Josh off at Mary's and were headed across town to the hotel.

'It was never going to be easy, Liv. I thought neutral territory might help to keep things in perspective.'

Liv gave a raw laugh. 'In other words, I can hardly make a show of us by getting up and walking out on you, can I?'

'Or throw your wine in my face.'

Please, heaven, it wouldn't come to that. Liv turned her head and addressed his profile. 'Josh is going to sense this tension between us, isn't he?'

She saw the muscle in his jaw tighten, before he said, 'Olivia, I'm back in Theatre at St Christopher's next Monday morning at seven-thirty. We have to get things resolved before I have to leave Bellreagh.'

There were only a smattering of patrons at the pub when they entered.

'They've done a nice job,' Liv said perfunctorily, taking a swift look around at the exposed brick walls and distressed pine furniture.

Seated, Adam pressed her about her preferences for wine and food.

'You order.' She shrugged. 'I don't much care what we eat.'

'Liv—'

'Steak and salad, then.' She made an impatient twitch with her hand. 'And a glass of the house red.'

An uneasy silence descended on them then, until the wine came. Adam peered into the dark red liquid for a second, before he said, 'I guess we should drink to a sane and fruitful discussion.'

Blinking rapidly, Liv ran the pad of her thumb across the raised pattern on her glass, before lifting it. 'We can only try, I suppose.'

Adam frowned. 'Are you willing to, Liv?'

Something like resentment stirred in Liv and she couldn't let go of it. 'I'd like to hear what you've come up with first.'

'OK.' Still holding his glass, Adam leant forward, his thumbs rubbing a circular motion on its base. 'I went to see Josh's class teacher and his school principal yesterday. It's obvious our son is a very bright student.'

'You should already know that,' Liv said defensively. 'I've always sent you copies of his school reports.'

'I realise that, but this is the first time I've had the opportunity for some face-to-face contact.' He paused and went on, slowly, 'I've also had a chat to Martin Burow at Kinross. They have an excellent choice of subjects. I want Josh to go there, Liv.'

Oh!

It was too hard and nightmarish to think about. But she had to. Adam was waiting, his face tilted towards her, his look expectant. 'What if he wants to go to high school here?' she said in a choked voice.

Adam lifted a shoulder dismissively. 'I've laid out a few options for him to think about.'

'Before you even discussed it with me?' she demanded, her voice rising.

Adam expelled a patience-gathering breath. 'Because you don't have an open mind about it, Liv. You'd prefer *never* to discuss it. You wish it would all just go away.' Picking up the piece of paper beside his plate, he frowned impatiently at it, rising to his feet. 'That's our number. Our meals are ready. Don't run out on me, Olivia,' he warned quietly. 'I don't care how long it takes, we're sorting this out tonight.'

Shakily, Liv lifted her glass of wine and gulped a mouthful. Her composure was shattering. Her fears had been proved right. Come hell or high water, Adam would get what he'd come for. She was going to lose her son.

Even though the steak was grilled to perfection, the salad extravagant and fresh, Liv could hardly bear to swallow any of it. She asked for another glass of wine and Adam rose courteously and got it for her.

Adam doubted he'd ever endured such a miserable evening in his life and every mouthful of food he'd taken had almost choked him. 'Talk to me, Livvy.'

Liv gave up the unequal struggle and pushed her plate aside. 'You always said you hated boarding school,' she accused, her voice low and hard. 'And now you're proposing to do exactly what your father did to you.'

'Josh wouldn't *be* a boarder. He'd live with me.'

'I won't let him be a latch-key kid, Adam. I won't!'

'For God's sake!' he bit out impatiently. 'I'll get a suitable housekeeper if I have to.'

'Or a suitable *wife,*' she challenged bitterly.

Adam made a rough sound of scorn. 'Whatever it takes.' He pushed a hand back through his dark hair in irritation. 'I want my son to attend my old school for his higher education, Olivia. I don't think that's unreasonable.'

Fighting back sick resentment, Liv swung up off her chair. 'Take me home!' she demanded, turning and marching stiff-backed out of the restaurant.

They all but slammed their way into the car. Instantly Adam pulled out his mobile phone. Liv listened unashamedly, not the least surprised that he'd called her mother.

'Would you mind keeping Josh overnight, Mary?' she heard him ask quietly. 'Liv and I still have a deal of talking to do. Thanks. One of us will collect him first thing so he can get ready for school. Sorry? Yes, I'll tell her. Bye.'

'What?' Liv huffed, as he ended the call.

Josh reached out his hand to start the car. 'Mary sends her love. And to tell you that things have a way of working out for the best.'

But the best for whom? Liv wondered bleakly, sitting in tear-blinded silence as they drove home.

Once home, she hung back while Adam unlocked the front door and waited for her to go through. 'I'm just going to wash my face,' she said in a flat, husky voice as she moved past him on the way to the bathroom.

'I'll make some tea,' he called after her.

Liv turned on the tap and, cupping her hands, bent over the basin and splashed cold water on her face over and over again. Straightening, she regarded her reflection in the mirror. She looked a mess and now her entire life was a mess.

As she plucked a towel from its rail and began to pat her skin dry, some of her mother's strength settled over her like a protective cloak. Liv's intake of breath was long and controlling. It would kill her but she'd just have to tough it out, gather herself up again and go on.

Without Josh.

* * *

He hadn't wanted to do this to her. Almost savagely, Adam grabbed the electric jug and sloshed the boiling water into the teapot. He ground out a harsh expletive as several droplets splashed onto his hand. Slamming the lid hurriedly onto the teapot, he swung back to the sink and let the cold water run on to the burn.

'Are you OK?' Liv came up quietly behind him.

'Clumsy,' he said shortly. 'Bit of a splash. Nothing to worry about.'

'If you say so.' She reached down the Cornish-blue mugs and poured the tea. Almost simultaneously, they each pulled out a chair and sat opposite each other.

'I never wanted to hurt you, Liv. Whatever else you think of me, please, believe that.'

She considered this and then conceded the truth with a barely perceptible nod. 'It's why you came back, though, isn't it?'

'It was a spontaneous decision,' he defended. He touched briefly on his conversation with his juvenile patient and how she'd inspired him to begin making what changes he could to his life.

'After speaking to Jade, I was suddenly hungry for the sight of my son.'

Liv felt her heart lurch painfully. 'I never realised… But things are changing, aren't they? Pretty soon you'll have him all to yourself and I'll be the one l-left behind.'

'Liv, don't. I hate this pain between us.' His voice had risen and tightened. *'Hate it!'*

'But you'll still take him from me, won't you?'

'Sweet God, Livvy…' His expression sharpened with anguish. 'Don't look at it in those terms. *Please.* We'll compromise. There'll be holidays. It won't be as bad as you think. And it's not about me getting my way. It's about Josh's future. The type of education he'll get at Kinross will be broader than anything he could hope for here. I'm not denigrating Bellreagh, but he has a place at one of the best schools in the state. Surely, whatever our differences, we'd be remiss not to let him take advantage of it.'

'He's a country kid through and through, Adam.'

'Of course he is. And Bellreagh has been a wonderful environment for him to grow up in.

But it's time to move on with the next phase of his growing up.'

Liv heard his voice as from a long way off, She lifted her gaze slowly to find his dark eyes, full of concern, searching hers. She hardened her heart. 'So, what's the next step, then?'

'There'll be an open day at Kinross in a couple of weeks' time. I'd like you to come to Sydney for it.'

'Fine,' Liv said stiffly. 'I'll arrange to take a few days of my leave.' She swallowed. 'Are we going to sit Josh down and tell him what's been decided?'

'I'd rather wait until you're feeling more settled about things. Perhaps we could just tell him you're coming to Sydney for a few days' holiday…'

'Looks like you've covered all the bases, then.' Her voice hardened. 'Was getting me into bed part of the plan?'

'No, it wasn't!' he denied, his eyes slashing her. 'I had no *plan,* as you put it, when I came here. What happened between us…' He stopped and shook his head. 'Maybe it was inevitable.'

'Then how sad for us.' Liv's heart dropped like a wounded bird. Because now they were left with nothing but hurt between them. And nowhere to go to ease that hurt. Abruptly, she pushed her chair back and rose to her feet. 'I think it might be better if you moved back to the motel tonight, Adam.'

'Whatever you want.' His mouth snapped shut, his tightly clamped lips a harsh line across his face. He jerked to his feet. 'I'll throw my stuff together now and get out of your way.'

After Adam had gone, Liv prowled through the house as if seeking signs that he was still there, that the evening hadn't been part of an awful nightmare. But each room echoed with stillness.

So this was really the end.

She blinked, angry to find her eyes filling. Then, turning on her heel, she went through to the kitchen, steeling herself to carry out the ordinary, mundane task of setting the table for breakfast. Automatically, she set out three placemats on the table, paused and bit her lip. As from tomorrow there would be only two for breakfast again. She shot the third placemat back into the drawer, biting her lips together to stop them trembling.

Feelings of loss and futility were suddenly like a frozen lump in her chest. It felt as though there was nothing of Adam left behind. Nothing of their lives together. Nothing of their loving.

The tears wouldn't be held back now. Wrapping her arms around her body tightly, as though she might break into pieces if she let go, Liv went to the loneliness of her big double bed and cried as though her heart would break.

CHAPTER ELEVEN

THE world could not be held back indefinitely.

Liv rose at her usual time and went to collect Josh from his grandmother's. Ignoring Mary's questioning little looks, she chivvied her son along and left before she broke down and told her mother everything.

Once home, Josh dashed inside, obviously wanting to share the early morning with his father. In the kitchen, Liv quashed her anxiety, automatically going through the motions of putting breakfast on the table.

In a few seconds Josh was back, arms folded, facing her. 'Where's Dad?'

Liv ground her bottom lip. 'He's moved back to the motel.'

'Did you guys have a fight?'

Liv could feel the accusation in his voice like

something tangible. 'More like a difference of opinion,' she said cautiously.

'About me?'

'It's more complicated than that, Josh. But we'll sort it out,' she promised.

Josh was having none of that. His frank young gaze pinned her. 'Does Dad want me to go to high school in Sydney?'

'Yes.' So much for Adam's request that they wait. But Liv wasn't about to prevaricate. Their son deserved the truth.

Josh threw himself down at the table and began shaking cereal into a bowl. 'Dad took me to see Kinross last time I went to stay with him in Sydney. It's got awesome sports facilities and computers and stuff.'

And neither of them had thought to tell her? 'Do you want to go there?' Liv's voice was barely audible.

'It's Dad's old school,' he said logically, as if that was an end to the matter.

Later, as Liv sat over her cup of tea, Josh asked diffidently, 'Won't you be late for work?'

She sent her son the ghost of a smile. 'I'm

going in late this morning.' She'd called and asked Suzy to cover for her. Heaven knew, she'd done the same for her colleague from time to time. 'I can drop you at school if you like. Or would you rather get the bus as usual?'

Josh checked the workmanlike watch on his wrist. 'I'll get the bus.'

Liv's heart was leapfrogging against her chest as she made her way into Casualty. She had no idea how she was going to get through the rest of the week.

She supposed she could try to keep out of Adam's orbit. But that would be difficult. He certainly believed in being hands-on in the department.

'You look like hell,' Suzie said in her usual forthright manner when Liv arrived at the nurses' station. 'What is it, a bug of some kind?'

Liv shrugged. 'Maybe. I felt headachy when I woke. Bit better now.'

'We've been fairly quiet anyhow.'

Liv's mouth turned down. 'Are you saying I wasn't missed?'

Suzy grinned. 'Only by Adam. He was looking for you earlier.'

Liv's heart did an odd tattoo. 'I imagine we'll catch up sooner or later,' she dismissed.

'Well, I'm about to sacrifice myself to the paperwork.' With a little flap of her hand Suzy said, 'Why don't you get a coffee, Liv? I'll yell if things hot up.'

What a good idea, Liv thought, ducking off towards the staffroom. She'd just spooned the instant coffee into a mug when a soft footfall behind her had her swinging round. Her throat dried. 'Adam.'

'Just checking in to see if you were OK.'

In a second she noticed his strained demeanour. Well, that makes two of us, she thought raggedly. 'Would you like a coffee?'

'Ah—yes, thanks. Why not?' He moved closer. 'Josh OK?'

'He knows about high school.' She rushed the words out. 'Well, he'd guessed something was up and asked me point blank. I couldn't lie to him.'

'Of course you couldn't.' Adam picked up his coffee from the benchtop.

'Why didn't you tell me you'd already taken him to look over Kinross?'

Adam's head went back at the accusatory lash in her voice. 'It wasn't meant to put pressure on him, Olivia. An open day just happened to coincide with Josh's visit. It was a bit of father-and-son time, that's all.'

Liv gave a raw laugh. 'Well, you certainly impressed him. He can't wait to follow in your footsteps.'

Adam felt as though he was fighting his way through quicksand. 'That's not a bad thing, is it?' he asked quietly.

No, it wasn't, and it was pointless going on and on about it. Where their son would complete his secondary schooling was a done deal.

Adam sighed. 'You want to make me the bad guy here, Liv, and I'm not. I'm just doing what any conscientious father would do—looking out for my son's welfare. And that's no slur on your parenting. I wish you could believe that.' He wrapped his fingers around his mug, as if seeking the warmth. 'How would you like to spend the last few days while I'm here?'

Liv hesitated. Crawling into bed and pulling the covers over her head seemed like a good option. 'Mum mentioned something about having us over for a family dinner.'

'That sounds good.'

'When are you leaving?'

His jaw tightened. 'Saturday morning.'

And today was Wednesday. She licked her lips. 'I'll ask Mum to make it tomorrow night, then, shall I?'

'If that suits Mary, yes, that'd be great.'

'She's going to miss Josh terribly.'

'Liv—give it up!' Adam's voice had sounded like that of a man almost driven beyond what he could endure. 'Emotional blackmail is not worthy of you. Anyhow, Mary's a realist. She'll understand that sometimes things have to change. Thanks for the coffee.' He held the mug aloft, before turning and walking out.

A flurry of minor accidents kept them busy until early afternoon. Liv worked mostly with their resident, Luci Chalmers, leaving Suzy to assist Adam. He knew what she was up to, of course. But she didn't care. Painting a bright smile on her face, she got on with what had to be done for their patients.

Then, suddenly, all her avoidance tactics were wasted. She and Adam were forced together by circumstances beyond their control. When the emergency call came, Liv went hurriedly to find him.

'What's up?' His dark brows twitched together impatiently.

'We've just received an emergency call from the ambulance base,' Liv said shortly. 'There's been an accident at Doonside. Reid's injured—seriously, from all accounts. And one of his stablehands, Aaron Glover. Something to do with one of the horses running amok. An ambulance has gone out but they've requested a doctor at the scene, stat.'

Adam swore softly. 'In that case, we'd better get out there.'

We? Liv felt prickles of alarm run up the back of her neck. 'You want me? I mean, Suzy is more than—'

'I want *you,* Olivia.' Adam's look was fierce. 'I trust you.'

And that seemed to say it all. An odd kind of compliment, Liv blinked uncertainly. 'I'll collect the emergency pack, then.'

Adam spun on his heel. 'I'll organise some cover. Meet me in the car park.'

On the road to Doonside, Adam put his foot down, hoping to cut the thirty-minute journey to twenty.

'I'd better make a couple of calls,' Liv said, taking out her mobile phone. First she called the school and asked that Josh be told to go to his grandmother's after school. Then she called Mary to make sure she'd be home when Josh arrived.

'It's quite a responsibility, rearing a kid, isn't it?' Adam flicked her a sideways glance. 'And you've done it so well, Liv.'

Liv's mouth tightened. Already he was speaking in the past tense. Determinedly, she set her mind on the emergency they were facing. 'What do you think might have happened at Doonside?'

'Reid works with brumbies.' Adam's voice was clipped. 'Use your imagination.'

Liv suppressed a shudder. The hooves of a

horse gone crazy with panic could wreak havoc on the human body. 'Does Reid wear a safety hat when he's working with them?'

'He was on Saturday when we were out there.'

'Thank heavens for that. Could it be the horse he was taming on Saturday that caused the trouble?'

'Angel? I hope not. Josh will be very upset about this,' he added gruffly.

They made it to Doonside in just under twenty minutes. Once through the entrance to the property, Adam drove straight to the yards. In a few seconds they were out of the car and running.

The injured men were lying some distance apart in the holding yard. 'Poor Kerry...' Liv glanced fearfully at the scene in front of them. Reid's wife had obviously brought blankets to cover both Reid and Aaron. Now she was huddled beside her husband, her head bowed as if she was already in mourning.

Liv's hand went to her throat. What an awful thing to happen. So much worse when you knew the people involved… She beat back the sick feeling of dread in her stomach. Whatever it took, she had to remain professional.

The ambulance had arrived barely seconds before them but Ben Vellacott had already made a snap assessment. 'It's grim, Doc. Aaron Glover's copped a hiding—fractured leg and iffy shoulder. But Reid's in a bad way. Could be spleen damage.'

'Right, I'll see him first.' Adam's expression became tight. 'You and Carol see what you can do for the other casualty, Ben. Don't hesitate to use your initiative. Liv?' He touched her shoulder. 'I'll need you with me.'

Reid looked very ill, his skin grey and glassy. Adam hunkered down beside his prostrate form.

'It was that black stallion.' Kerry's face was pinched. She looked at Adam with a terrible kind of resignation in her eyes. 'He's going to die, isn't he?'

'Kerry…' Adam dropped his hand on the woman's shoulder and squeezed. 'We'll do everything possible to see that doesn't happen. Just let us get to work—please?'

'Sorry.' Kerry rose hastily and backed away.

Adam began probing for a pulse on the injured man's wrist. He shook his head. 'Barely there. Get a BP reading, Liv.' In a second he was whipping a torch out of the trauma pack. 'Pupils are all over the place.' His gaze swung in a querying arc to Liv.

She shook her head. 'Seventy over forty.' They both knew they had a crisis of mammoth proportions on their hands. Very likely Reid was bleeding internally. Liv's hands moved swiftly to loosen Reid's jeans to enable Adam to palpate the stockman's stomach.

'We've got trouble.' Adam's response was flat. 'He's hard all over. Get a line in, Liv. We'll push Haemaccel into him and hope we can stave off disaster until we get him to the OR.'

With a last grim look at his patient Adam shot upright. Pulling his mobile from his back pocket, he hit a number on the speed dial and waited to be connected.

'Suzy? Adam. Could you alert Theatres, please? I'm bringing in a forty-plus male, suspected ruptured spleen. The patient is bleeding

out rapidly. I'll need to do an emergency lapa-
rotomy. Round up all available O-neg blood
and we'll cross-match on arrival.'

'Anaesthetic could be a problem,' Suzy said
calmly. 'Nick is already in Theatre with Dr Tran.
We've had an RTA emergency since you left.
What do you want to do?'

Adam pressed the heel of his hand against his
forehead, thinking. 'Ask Tim Crossingham to
scrub and wait for me. He's had some experience and I can guide him until Nick can take
over. And, Suzy, have the team ready to meet us
in Resus. And haul in whatever theatre staff you
can to stand by. I'll approve the overtime.'

Liv felt a swirl of nervous tension in her
stomach. Ideally, Reid should have been air-
lifted to Sydney. But the time factor was critical:
he needed emergency surgery. Thank heaven,
Adam had the skills. But what about poor
Kerry? A lump formed in Liv's throat. Was she
about to lose her soulmate?

'Back in a tick.' Adam grabbed his case and
sprinted across to where Aaron was lying. 'Well
done, guys.' He cast a swift, discerning look

over the injured man. Aaron's shoulder had been supported in a sling and he'd been placed on oxygen.

'What do you reckon about the leg, Doc?' Ben was at Adam's elbow. 'Fractured NOF?'

'Undoubtedly. Would you get a doughnut dressing around that protruding bone, please? He's going to need an open reduction and internal fixation. We'll Medivac him straight through to St Vincent's.'

'We're one jump ahead of you there,' Ben said. 'I've already called the base. Chopper's on its way. I figured you'd have enough on your plate with Reid.'

'Good man. We'll need to stabilise Aaron for the journey in that case. Let's get him hooked up to some normal saline for starters and I'll whip in a jab of morphine to tide him over until he gets to hospital. Then we have to step on it, guys.'

'I'll back the ambulance up closer so we can lessen the trauma for Reid's transfer,' Carol came in with quiet authority.

'Right.' Adam pulled in a breath and let it go. 'Kerry can ride with you in the cabin. Liv and

I will monitor Reid. Ben, you assume responsibility for Aaron and see him safely transferred to the chopper. And afterwards, if you wouldn't mind driving my car back to town?' Adam hauled his keys from the deep pocket of his cargo pants and tossed them across to the other's outstretched hand.

The journey along the stretch of country road was the stuff of nightmares. 'I'll try to make it as smooth as I can for the patient,' Carol had said. 'But there are some dips and bumps I'm not going to be able to avoid. The maintenance on this stretch of road is appalling.'

'Don't take your eyes off him, Liv.' Adam's expression was strained. 'How's his BP doing?'

'Hardly there, but he's hanging on. Are you going to take blood?'

Adam snapped on a new pair of gloves. 'If I can find a vein to give me anything. I feel like I'm depriving him of what little he's got. But, hell, we've got to have something to at least try for a cross-match.'

'How on earth is Kerry going to cope?' Liv's voice cracked.

'You know her better than I do, Liv. Is there family to support her?'

'Don't think so. Well, not in Bellreagh at least. Kerry and Reid are fairly private. I do know Reid's been divorced. Kerry is his second wife.'

'Well, whatever the situation, we can only do the best we can for Reid,' Adam summed up heavily. 'And just pray it's enough.'

Reid was rushed into Resus on their arrival at the hospital.

'Pull out all the stops, guys! We can't lose this one.' Adam began stripping off on his way to the basin. He elbowed the taps on. 'We've got to get him as stable as possible before surgery. Dr Chalmers!' He spoke sharply over his shoulders to A and E's resident. 'Blood's critical. Put another line in the patient's right arm and cannulas in both feet in case we need them.'

With quick precision Liv cut through Reid's clothes. 'Theatre gown, please,' she snapped to Bianca. 'And, Cait, be ready with a space blanket. He's very cold.'

'Right, let's go!' Adam was jamming on a

theatre cap as he spoke. 'And bring the life pack, please. We might have to zap him on the way.'

Liv did her best to offer comfort to Kerry. She'd taken her through to the sunroom and got them both a cup of tea.

'What will Dr Westerman do?' Kerry had got control of herself and now held her mug of tea tightly in front of her at the small table.

Liv explained as simply as she could. 'He has to try and stop the bleeding, Kerry. That will be his biggest concern.'

'And if he c-can't?' Kerry's eyes looked suddenly too big for her face.

'We won't dwell on that. Adam is a highly skilled surgeon. He won't give up lightly.'

'He's your ex-husband, isn't he?' Kerry spoke quietly but Liv registered the depth of concern in her regard.

'Yes. He's here from Sydney for a couple of weeks to spend time with Josh. And covering for Dr McGregor while he's on leave.'

'Has it been...difficult? I mean, working

together so closely must make you…well, somewhat vulnerable?'

Liv's hands curled into fists on her lap. That wasn't even the half of it. 'We've managed,' she said with a little twitch of her shoulder.

'Reid's been divorced. We've only been together a few years.'

'You seem very close.'

Kerry's little nod was forlorn and it tugged at Liv's heart. 'If I lose him, I don't know what I'd—'

'You mustn't think like that,' Liv said bracingly. 'We only allow positive thoughts in this place. Now, is there anyone we can call for you? Anyone who would want to know about Reid's accident?'

Kerry rubbed at a little spot on the table. 'There are his daughters. They're fourteen and sixteen. They live in Sydney with their mother.' She swallowed thickly. 'Sadly, Reid doesn't have much of a relationship with them. They came to Doonside a couple of times for school holidays. They stayed only a few days each time. They don't really like the bush—or maybe it's me they don't like.'

'Is Reid in contact with them?' Liv asked gently.

Kerry blinked a bit. 'He tries. But it's difficult when they're so far away. I think it's quite tragic…' She paused. 'I mean, he's their dad and they're part of him. They could add so much to one another's lives if only they could work it out.' She shook her head. 'They're missing out on such a lot. And if their father dies—they'll have lost their chance for ever.'

Liv's insides wrenched as shades of her own situation rose up to challenge her. 'I realise it's awkward but perhaps you *should* let the girls know about their father.'

Kerry gave a brittle laugh. 'They won't want to come here!'

'They wouldn't have to,' Liv explained. 'As soon as Reid is stable, he'll be transferred to an intensive care unit in Sydney. You'll be able to go with him in the air ambulance.'

Kerry's fingers had stilled but now they started their rubbing again. 'So the girls could see him there—that's if they wanted to.'

Liv nodded.

'I'll call them, then.' Kerry's voice firmed. 'It would be wrong of me not to.'

'Make your call from Sister's office.' Liv touched the other woman on the shoulder as she rose to her feet. 'You'll be quite private there.'

While Kerry was telephoning her stepdaughters, Liv took the opportunity to call Mary. It was well after Liv should have come off duty but she hadn't wanted to leave Kerry in her worried state.

'When will you be home?' Mary asked promptly.

Liv explained about Kerry. 'I wondered if you could keep Josh for a while longer, Mum.'

'No, Olivia. I'm afraid I can't.'

'Oh.' Liv was taken aback. 'Is there a problem?'

'There will be if this lad doesn't get home where he belongs. He's aware things between you and his father are strained and he's fretting about Reid. He needs to know what's going on.'

'All right…' Liv massaged her forehead with one hand, as if to clear her thinking process. 'I'll be over as soon as I can and take Josh home. I'm sorry it's been hard on you, Mum.'

Mary clicked her tongue. 'It's your son you

should be thinking about, Livvy, not me. I'll tell him you're on your way.'

Liv made her way back to the staffroom to collect her things. She'd have to tell Kerry she was leaving…

'Liv, don't you have a home to go to?' Mike Townsend, the charge for the late shift, poked his head in the door.

Suddenly Liv felt as though she was being attacked from all sides for simply being a caring person. She brought her chin up defensively. 'I've been looking after Kerry Charlton. It's hardly been a picnic for her, with her husband fighting for his life. Someone's got to be here for her.'

'We're *all* here for her,' Mike pointed out gruffly. He came into the room, propping himself against the bank of lockers and folding his arms. There was concern in his eyes. 'You can't be all things to all people, Liv. Especially in this job. You should be with your son. All the lads in Reid's troop are going to be hit pretty hard by this.'

Liv bit down on her bottom lip. After her mother's censure, Mike's words only added to her feelings of having completely let her son down in some way. She moistened her lips. 'Kerry's trying to contact Reid's daughters. I gather it's not an easy relationship.'

'I'll keep an eye on her. Meanwhile, home— OK?'

'I'm going.' Liv gave in with a resigned little roll of her eyes. 'But if you hear anything… I mean, for Josh's sake?'

'I'll keep you posted,' he promised. 'Now scoot.'

'Is Reid going to die?' Josh asked with the artlessness of youth. They were on their way home from Mary's.

'He's very seriously injured,' Liv said carefully. 'Dad will do everything he can as a surgeon to save him.'

Josh slumped in his seat. 'But maybe even Dad can't.'

'No, Josh. Maybe even Dad can't.' Liv heard her voice thin and clogged. 'We'll all just have to stick together for the next little while, won't we?'

'Granny and I said a prayer together.'

Liv's fingers turned into a while-knuckled grip on the steering-wheel. Somehow they had to get through this dreadful time.

Once home, Josh threw his backpack onto the floor.

'Have you done your homework?' Liv asked gently.

He shrugged. 'I did it at Granny's.'

'Well, hop in for your shower, then, hmm? I'll get some dinner going.'

'I'm not hungry.'

'I'm not either, but we have to try and eat something.' With a ragged sigh, Liv opened the kitchen window and let in the cool air of early evening. 'What about your favourite—egg and chips?'

She watched as his mouth moved in the half-smile so like his father's. 'Yeah, OK.'

While Josh was in the shower, Liv began preparations for the simple meal, one ear listening for the phone. But deep down she knew it was far too soon to expect any news from Mike, except if Reid had—She stopped her thoughts going along that path and brought herself up with a jolt.

'When is Dad going back to Sydney?' Josh savoured his last chip. They'd sat side by side on the sofa and eaten their informal meal off trays in front of the fire.

'On Saturday morning.'

'It won't be the same when he's gone, will it?' Josh returned his tray to the coffee-table, then propped his chin on his hand.

Liv sought desperately for the right response. 'Well, it'll be back to just you and me. But next year you'll be with Dad all the time.'

'But *you* won't be there.'

Oh, Josh. Liv felt as though a huge hand had grabbed her insides and was squeezing the life out of them. She swallowed the lump in her throat. 'Honey, it's just the way things have turned out. But there'll be holidays and I'll see you lots.'

Her son didn't say anything. Instead, after a breathless little pause, he lunged towards his mother, burying his face against her breast and crying as though his heart would break.

Liv hugged him, rocking him gently and agonising about the terrible heartache she and Adam had brought on their son. After a while, when he'd become quiet, she gave him a comforting squeeze. 'Hey—things will seem better tomorrow. Please, God, we'll have some good news about Reid and we'll have a really good talk to Dad and sort things out—like when we'll see each other. And that will all be something to look forward to, won't it?'

'I guess...' Josh sat up, took a steadying breath and squared his shoulders. 'Don't tell Dad I howled,' he mumbled.

Liv gathered him to her again and pressed a kiss to his damp hair. 'Our secret. But it's OK to cry, sweetheart. Now, would you like to watch a video?' It was getting towards his bedtime but what the heck? It was hardly a normal kind of evening.

'Nah.' Josh scrubbed his nose with his sleeve. 'I'll just read my books. If Dad calls about Reid...'

'I'll let you know,' Liv promised gently. 'Even if you're asleep, I'll wake you. Deal?'

Josh nodded and returned his mother's high-five salute a bit half-heartedly before he wandered off towards his bedroom.

Watching him go, Liv felt fat tears spilling down her cheeks and brushed them away angrily. What kind of parents were they? Not very good, she chastised herself ruthlessly. It had shocked her through and through to see her usually stoic child reduced to such vulnerability.

She took a breath so deep it hurt. Surely, surely, there had to be a better way…

It was another two hours before Mike rang. 'Liv?'

'Yes! Yes, Mike.' She yanked in a shaking breath. 'Do you have any news?'

'Reid's holding his own.' Mike sounded slightly guarded. 'Took some sorting apparently. His spleen was ruptured and there was a tear in the bowel as well. He's in ICU now and stabilising. If there are no complications tonight, Adam thinks they'll airlift him to the Prince William tomorrow.'

'And Adam—is he OK?'

'Actually, he looked done in. I'd break out the Scotch, Liv. I reckon he'll need one when he gets home.'

Except he wasn't coming *home*. Liv felt her composure shattering. He wasn't coming home at all. Instead, he was going to the sterile, cold anonymity of a motel room.

CHAPTER TWELVE

LIV sat on the sofa in a kind of daze.

Josh had been only lightly asleep and had flown out to the lounge room when the phone had rung to hear the news Liv relayed from Mike.

'So Reid will be OK?' Tousled-haired, Josh blinked up at her.

'It'll take a while. But, yes, he should be OK.' Liv reached out and hugged her son briefly. 'See, your prayers were answered. Sleep now.' She pushed him gently towards the hallway.

But she felt wide awake herself, the nerves of her stomach tied in a thousand knots. When a soft knock came on the front door, she lifted her head sharply towards the sound and then went to answer it.

As she opened the door, the sensor light on the

porch outlined the figure standing outside. 'Adam!' She scooped in a sharp breath.

'I'm whacked,' he said, and looked at her. Light flared briefly behind him, accentuating the deep grooves of weariness in his lean face. 'And I had to talk to you.'

Liv drew him inside and tried to gather her scattered thoughts. 'Mike Townsend called,' she told him gently. 'Reid will pull through…?'

Adam's mouth tightened. 'Just about. His insides were shot. Took some sorting.'

And that, Dr Westerman, Liv thought silently, is the understatement of the decade. 'Come and sit down.' She gestured towards the sofa. 'The fire's nearly out but I could—'

'Liv, it's fine,' Adam told her, sinking gratefully into the comfortable cushioned seat. He tipped his head back, his eyes sweeping her in a brief caress. 'Any of that Scotch left?'

'Nearly all of it.' Liv was glad to have something practical to do. 'I'll bring the bottle.'

Once in the kitchen, she was able to suck in a few calming breaths. She assembled ice cubes and glasses, deciding she'd join him in a small drink, and placed them all on a tray. 'Here we are.' She put the tray on the coffee-table and then sat down beside him. Leaning over, she made the drinks, Adam's a much stronger one than hers.

He downed it in a couple of swallows, feeling the warmth of the liquor hit his insides like a ridge of fire. 'I thought I'd lost him a dozen times, Livvy.' He stared down broodingly into his glass.

'But your skills brought him back,' Liv affirmed quietly. 'And Josh's prayers.'

His mouth lifted in a brief half-smile. 'They must have kicked in when I was about halfway through. How is our boy?'

Liv hesitated. 'Relieved. He was upset this evening, but not just about Reid.'

One dark brow flicked upwards. 'Tell me.'

'Later. Why don't I make you something to eat?'

He shook his head. 'I don't know whether I—'

'Scrambled eggs and toast,' Liv decided firmly. 'It'll only take a minute.' She was gone in a flash.

When she returned to the lounge, Adam was

lying back, his head burrowed into the cushions, his eyes closed. She swallowed, his vulnerability almost her undoing. 'Adam?' she called gently.

His eyes snapped open. In a bone-weary gesture, he lifted his arms and stretched. 'I must have dozed off. That looks good, thanks.'

'You're welcome. Tuck in. I'll make some tea.'

When she brought in the tea, she saw Adam had almost finished his eggs. She gave a tentative smile. 'You were hungry after all.'

'Mmm.' He gave her a dry look from under half-closed lids. 'You know me too well.'

She took her place beside him once again. After a moment, heavy with silence, she said, 'I'm beginning to think we hardly know one another at all.'

Adam seemed to have some idea where she was coming from. He was leaning forward, his mug of tea clasped between his hands. 'We can't rewrite the past, Liv.'

'No. But we can try to change the future,' she responded, her voice coming out low and a bit uneven. 'I've had a long time to think about things this evening and I've come to a decision.'

Adam placed his mug back on the table and swung to face her. His eyes were wary, the dawning hope in them quickly suppressed. 'About what?'

'This family. Belatedly, I've realised Josh needs both of us close by to feel secure.'

He snorted. 'I could have told you that. I just wish I could have made it happen.'

'But we can, Adam,' she said earnestly. 'We *can*.'

He was silent for so long her heart almost stopped but then he smiled, a shaky unsteady smile that he couldn't hold onto. He pressed his lips together and nodded. 'And I've thought of a way to do it. It came to me right after Reid's surgery. I can work here. The hospital can always use another general surgeon. At least I'll be around for my son, and that means more to me than anything else.'

Liv stared in disbelief. 'And you'd give up your work at St Christopher's, a lifestyle you love—everything—just like that?'

'Well, not quite. It will take a bit of time to arrange. But, yes, Livvy, I'll do whatever it takes to keep the semblance of a family. Josh can go to high school here. I can't leave you behind, desperate and unhappy without your son.'

'Oh, Adam...' Liv blinked the sudden tears away from her eyes. 'That's what I did to you.'

His mouth tightened. 'We were little more than adolescents. What did we know about life? You did what you thought was best at the time.'

'Well, I'm older now and hopefully a bit wiser.' She stopped and sniffed and blinked a bit. 'And I'm sorry, but I can't let you give up everything you've worked so hard for. We have to keep this family together, so *I'll* come to Sydney. Heaven knows, there are enough hospitals crying out for senior nurses. I can get an apartment and maybe Josh can come to me on alternate weekends or something...'

'You'd do that?' He looked at her his eyes dark with bemusement. 'But you hate the city.'

'Not any more. I'm not the little country mouse I once was.' She paused and then said, 'I'd walk through fire for Josh's well-being. And it seems to me his well-being is with us as a family.'

'Together but not really together…'

Liv interlinked her fingers and pressed them against her chest. 'At least we'd be in the same city. So…anything could happen.'

'Like what?' He lifted his eyes briefly, just long enough for her to see the hope in them before he looked away. Was she really saying they had a future? Together? But it was such a giant step into the unknown. And they had a pile of baggage a train couldn't knock over. And yet he clung to the tiny flame of optimism that flickered in his heart. 'What are you saying, Livvy?'

'I think we should stop messing about and find out what's really keeping us apart.'

'And perhaps, if we moved a bit closer…?' So saying, he held out his arm in invitation and folded her in against him.

'Maybe it's because we've been living miles away from each other,' Liv said tentatively. 'The telephone is no substitute for being able to touch.'

'No. But on the other hand, I'd hate it if we got back together and hurt each other all over again,' Adam contributed soberly.

'But surely we've moved on from there, haven't we? I mean, we still fancy each other…'

His eyes darkened. 'I think that's a given,' he growled.

'So, are you going to let me come to Sydney, then?' she coaxed, folding her hand across his and stroking his knuckles.

Adam was silent for a long time. 'As long as you and Josh move in with me.'

Her heart trembled but she was too aware of the power of his words to be anything but cautious. 'If that's what you truly want?'

'More than anything.' He put his hand behind her head, drawing her forward, closer and closer, until his mouth was playing with hers, making her shiver. 'Take me back, Livvy. Give our marriage another chance.'

'We're not actually married any more.'

'That can be easily remedied. Will you trust me to make you happy?'

Liv knew she had no choice. She loved him too much not to trust him, but she also had belief in her heart.

'As long as you trust me to make you happy

too.' Liv curled into him, embracing him. 'It's taken me a long time to realise it—but I love you, Adam. So much.'

He stroked her cheek. 'And I love you, Livvy. I've never stopped.'

'Oh, help.' Liv felt tears again. 'I don't know how I could ever have left you…'

'Hush.' He held her tighter and they were quiet for a while until Liv stirred and asked, 'Way back then, Adam, why didn't you take the money your father offered? You said something about not being able to accept his conditions.'

'That's history.' The corners of his mouth compressed determinedly. 'Leave it there, Liv.'

She chewed her lip. 'We're starting over, clean slates. I think you have to tell me.'

'Even if it hurts?'

Liv hesitated, the languid softness of her limbs evaporating abruptly. Should she let it go? As Adam had said, it was over and done with. But this was to be their brave new beginning, a world with no more shadows of the past hanging over them. 'I think so,' she said slowly. 'We need to start afresh.'

'All right.' Adam's shoulders lifted in a long sigh. 'My father offered me an obscene amount of money to leave medicine and join him in the family business. He was going to buy us a house in Bellreagh with all the trappings.'

'He wanted you to give up your dream?' Liv was appalled.

'My father didn't see it like that, Liv. For his own self-image, he wanted his son to carry on in his footsteps. He never wanted me around when I was a child but then I grew up and I seemed bright enough to be trotted out as an adjunct to his ego.' He laughed rawly. 'He never understood me but I always knew where he was coming from. He never did anything for altru- istic motives.'

Instead of feeling hurt, Liv felt suddenly, vi- olently angry. 'He tried to bribe you!'

Adam snorted. 'And I thought about it for all of ten seconds.'

'And back then I thought you were just being stubborn and bloody-minded for not taking the money,' Liv said faintly.

A beat of silence.

'I felt bad about it for months afterwards,' Adam confessed. 'Wondering whether I'd made a huge mistake, whether I could have left medicine and perhaps come back to it later on.'

Liv circled her hands around his neck. 'The only mistake you made was not telling me. Were you afraid I'd try to talk you into it?'

'Possibly—probably. I don't know. In those days I was drunk with fatigue most of the time. Perhaps I was just incredibly selfish about my own needs.'

'Shh. We were both young,' Liv said softly. 'Being self-centred goes with the territory. You don't think our actions have harmed Josh, do you, Adam?' she asked abruptly.

'We've bent over backwards not to let that happen.' He lifted his hand to trace the outline of her lips. 'He seems pretty together to me.'

She stilled his hand and kissed the tips of his fingers. 'He'll be over the moon tomorrow when we tell him our news.'

'Together?' Adam prompted huskily.

'First thing in the morning.'

'So, I'm staying the night, then?'

'With me…in my bed.' She gave him a long, tantalising kiss full of the confidence their newly reclaimed commitment had given her. 'You'll have to check out of the motel again.'

Adam groaned. 'They'll think I'm mad.'

'Do you care?'

Adam's hand drifted to the soft underswell of her breast and began stroking. And he found he didn't care at all. His wife and son were back in his life.

They were together. For ever. A family at last.

MEDICAL ROMANCE™

Large Print

Titles for the next six months…

November

HIS HONOURABLE SURGEON	Kate Hardy
PREGNANT WITH HIS CHILD	Lilian Darcy
THE CONSULTANT'S ADOPTED SON	Jennifer Taylor
HER LONGED-FOR FAMILY	Josie Metcalfe
MISSION: MOUNTAIN RESCUE	Amy Andrews
THE GOOD FATHER	Maggie Kingsley

December

MATERNAL INSTINCT	Caroline Anderson
THE DOCTOR'S MARRIAGE WISH	Meredith Webber
THE DOCTOR'S PROPOSAL	Marion Lennox
THE SURGEON'S PERFECT MATCH	Alison Roberts
THE CONSULTANT'S HOMECOMING	Laura Iding
A COUNTRY PRACTICE	Abigail Gordon

January

THE MIDWIFE'S SPECIAL DELIVERY	Carol Marinelli
A BABY OF HIS OWN	Jennifer Taylor
A NURSE WORTH WAITING FOR	Gill Sanderson
THE LONDON DOCTOR	Joanna Neil
EMERGENCY IN ALASKA	Dianne Drake
PREGNANT ON ARRIVAL	Fiona Lowe

MILLS & BOON®

Live the emotion

1006 LP 2P P1 Medical

MEDICAL ROMANCE™

Large Print

February

THE SICILIAN DOCTOR'S PROPOSAL — Sarah Morgan
THE FIREFIGHTER'S FIANCÉ — Kate Hardy
EMERGENCY BABY — Alison Roberts
IN HIS SPECIAL CARE — Lucy Clark
BRIDE AT BAY HOSPITAL — Meredith Webber
THE FLIGHT DOCTOR'S ENGAGEMENT — Laura Iding

March

CARING FOR HIS CHILD — Amy Andrews
THE SURGEON'S SPECIAL GIFT — Fiona McArthur
A DOCTOR BEYOND COMPARE — Melanie Milburne
RESCUED BY MARRIAGE — Dianne Drake
THE NURSE'S LONGED-FOR FAMILY — Fiona Lowe
HER BABY'S SECRET FATHER — Lynne Marshall

April

RESCUE AT CRADLE LAKE — Marion Lennox
A NIGHT TO REMEMBER — Jennifer Taylor
THE DOCTORS' NEW-FOUND FAMILY
— Laura MacDonald
HER VERY SPECIAL CONSULTANT — Joanna Neil
A SURGEON, A MIDWIFE: A FAMILY — Gill Sanderson
THE ITALIAN DOCTOR'S BRIDE — Margaret McDonagh

MILLS & BOON®
Live the emotion

1006 LP 2P P2 Medical